Trapped

written and illustrated by

Blaine Turner

The Dollhouse Trilogy

Book 1 - **Trapped**
Book 2 - **Captive**
Book 3 - **Embraced**

Trapped

Copyright © 2006, 2008

by

Blaine P. Turner

This little book is dedicated with love to
my daughter Krista.

~1~
A Simpler Time

Will you join me in an amazing tale?

It was a simpler time. At least that is what everyone is so fond of saying now that we've entered the modern age of computer games, MP3 players, and DVDs. "Oh, our days are so hectic now," we say. But just being busy doesn't mean that our lives are rich and rewarding. Or even fun. Just look at the ants and how busy they are. Why they're constantly out getting groceries, caring for the little ones, cleaning house or fighting off a myriad of enemies. Yet they have no brains to speak of and go through life acting on simple impulse. Perhaps like us nowadays, a little bit? Busy, busy, busy. Don't you think?

Now this is a story of how I grew up in the "simpler times," in the decade after the great World War II. We were called "baby boomers" because at war's end all the soldiers came home and had babies with their wives. It was as simple as that. But for me, a small boy, life was not simple at all. Well, for instance, insects in my world could talk, even make sarcastic jokes, and if they didn't have wings themselves, they would pilot plastic airplanes around my room. These airplanes were mostly bombers or fighters because there was a great and deadly war being waged between the good cowboys and the bad army men. The horses and barnyard animals always sided with the cowboys, but the dinosaurs backed the toy soldiers. Yet, the insects I'd brought into the house just wandered about the battlefield disinterestedly and eventually I too grew a bit disillusioned with such childish battles. Finally I left this entire display of foolishness to my baby brother James. Now James was much more spirited in his war games than I, even to the point of tearing arms off dolls, wings off beetles, and using real fire to melt dinosaurs. I'm sure you would never do such horrible things, even in make believe. Would you?

Talking insects? If you think this is a bit fantastic, just wait 'till I tell you how I rescued baby James from them. And my little sister Katherine as well. Actually James wasn't a baby at the time but he still acted like one. And my sister, though a bit younger than I, was always pretending to be a grown up lady, and in many respects, I suppose she really was. Ours is a fanciful but true adventure from which we were lucky to return alive. So without further ado, let us begin. Will you come back with me in time? Will you put away your other thoughts and playthings? Will you close your eyes? If you get scared you can hold my hand, or even sit in my lap, but whatever you do, don't cover my eyes, for I need to see where we're going or we'll get hopelessly lost in this book forever. To help us see things more clearly, I've drawn a few pictures. I'm not a real artist but I hope you enjoy them anyway.

~2~
Aunt Clara's House

It all started with the regular visits to our great aunt Clara's house for Sunday midday dinners. On Sundays we three children were already cleaned and dressed up for church, so Mom and Dad didn't have to attend to that chore more than once in a weekend. Me, I hated wearing my silly clip-on tie. You could see how it hung from my collar with fakey metal strips. Every once in a while it would just fall off all by itself and everyone would laugh inwardly at me. To tell you the truth, I would have much preferred my dad's real tie, which I'd see him tying every morning at the bathroom mirror. By then I was certainly old enough to wear a real tie. James could have my clip-on, although you'd have to tie it on him with a string to keep it there. He hated to dress up even more than I. Katherine, on the other hand, loved her frilly dresses and shiny patent leather shoes. When Mom wore a hat she had to have one too. Dad always wore a brown fedora but we boys wouldn't be caught dead in one, not having heard of Indiana Jones yet.

Whenever we arrived at Aunt Clara's house I always stopped to look up at its massive stonework, covered partly in ivy. There were bird nests in it and if you were lucky you could spot a bird flying out. I had always meant to remember the exact places so I could get a ladder and find the eggs, but it seems I would always get distracted by even greater adventures in the back yard.

"Oh how grand to see you again, William," Aunt Clara would always chirp as we entered the stately front door. I would smile sweetly, but as soon as politely possible duck out through the screen door in back to the huge formal garden with an artificial fish pond. There were real goldfish in it, but I would be studying the habits of frogs under the lily pads.

My little brother James would invariably dart past my legs and be out to his favorite climbing maple where he'd hide in its leaves until dinner.

Katherine, on the other hand, would be so pleased to see Aunt Clara and all her amazing lady things that she would literally jump up and down on her white, spindly legs. Why there were antique chairs standing beside stately tables with ornate music boxes and graceful lamps on them, attached to frayed wire cords. There were pictures of frighteningly stern people on every wall and mirrors with wavy glass which distorted her childish face when she looked into them. There was a great, red brick fireplace with shiny brass andirons and a quaint looking dustbin. And this was only the living room.

Down the narrow hall in the den were shelves and whatnots filled with all sorts of intriguing books and artifacts. Dominating one wall, on the floor beside a cozy loveseat stood a grand old radio. It was bigger than most TVs today but of course it had only one small lighted dial and four round knobs to amuse oneself with. James had once pulled a knob all the way off and came crying to me with it. I told him how serious this was and how Grandpa had died fooling around with electricity that way. Actually I had no idea how Grandpa had got his heart attack. Certainly it was *not* from tugging at radio knobs. Nevertheless, James was trembling as I led him back into the den and carefully replaced the knob, which slid on all too easily. So I proceeded to tweak it a bit here and there until James was suitably impressed with my superior abilities.

"You won't tell, will you?" he asked, his voice small and quavering.

"Not if you obey me the rest of your natural life!" I replied sternly, and he shrunk quietly away.

Katherine most enjoyed the powder room next door. It was elegant, extravagant, no bigger than a closet and had dark red wallpaper with a fancy swirly design in real blue velvet that you couldn't help but run your hands across. The toilet had an ornate solid gold handle and the water in it matched the blue of the wallpaper. She was sure there were fairies living in the two wonderfully faceted chandeliers hanging in front of the regal mirror with etched glass borders. The tiny room smelled heavily of floral soap which we children were afraid to use. We were also afraid to touch the exquisite embroidered guest towels, so we always wiped our hands on our sleeves, or on James if he was within reach.

On one particular day, and for no particular reason, Katherine decided to take a chance and venture upstairs. Now no one had expressly forbidden this, but she had never been exactly invited up there either. Still, the rich mahogany banister and dark shoe-warn stairs felt so inviting to her small hands and feet that she started up on all fours, wary as a cat. Every so often she would peer down over her shoulder, but no adult ever came into view to yell at her. Eventually she reached the halfway point, turned and proud of herself, sat on the step, surveying the panoramic view of everything it afforded.

Suddenly there was Mother yelling, "Oh, there you are Katherine, come down and find the boys. It's time for dinner. And don't get your dress dirty on those stairs. Stand up straight. Don't brush your dress against the wall. Hold on to the banister. Hurry up, we don't have all day. Stop craning your neck. Walk like a lady."

Poor Katherine shot past Mother and lunged out the screen door yelling for her brothers. "I could have done that," trailed Mother, "GO and find them."

"James, get out of that tree," Katherine shrieked, peering straight up into the sun-flecked leaves. "Dinner's ready. Where's William? He's in big doodoo if he's late."

Of course I wasn't late. In fact I was able to sneak back into the house and be in my seat before my siblings realized I was nowhere to be found in the backyard. Or in the front yard either.

Arriving late to the table, James seemed insensible to my clever, but misguided practical joke. Katherine, however, gave me a long cold stare as she slipped into her chair and picked at her salad.

So it went on for several Sunday visits, with us boys adventuring in the back yard and little Katherine inching further and further up the stairs to the second floor. After a good many visits she discovered there was amazingly a *third* floor to the house. At least there was a stairway going up to somewhere and a small landing at the top. With increasing boldness and agility, one day she was able to make it all the way to the top before the call to dinner came. In front of her stood a massive, sinister looking door with a very out-of-date round crystal doorknob. If she looked closely, she could see pieces of her turned up nose and deep blue eyes reflected in its facets. Most intriguing, however, was the fact that the door had a great wide antique keyhole, through which she could plainly see part of an old bed, a bureau with a teacup on it, and an old rocker. "Grandmother must have lived here before she died," she conjectured. "I've heard she was quite insane. Perhaps she isn't dead at all, but asleep in that old bed. Bravely, and perhaps foolishly she gave the knob a turn but the door was securely locked. There was, however an unmistakable rustling noise coming from inside and Katherine's eyes widened and her hand froze on the knob as if it had turned to ice.

Then at this very instant came the piercing "dinner" call from below and somehow she was able to bound down all those steps without touching even one, so it seemed to her.

"My, my," said Aunt Clara at the table, "Katherine, you look like you've seen a ghost!"

"Oh no," returned Katherine politely, "I've just been hopping and skipping about."

"Such a pretty little girl," said Aunt Clara, addressing no one in particular, "she has her mother's nose and mouth, but my sister's light hair and dark blue eyes."

Katherine knew she was referring to her grandmother, the very grandmother who, for all she knew was still residing upstairs.

~3~
The Third Floor

O n the next visit, Katherine made straight for the keyhole and everything looked just the same, except alarmingly, the teacup was on the floor, broken into several pieces. "Now if Aunt Clara had done that, she would most certainly have cleaned it up immediately," she thought. "So if Aunt Clara didn't break the teacup then who did?" As always, the door was locked so once again she descended the stairs with her thoughts quite unsettled indeed.

Running her hand across the balusters on the stairs and then along the wainscot in the hall, she was led to a small room opposite the den occupied only by a roll top desk, a swivel chair and a floor lamp. Curiosity getting the better of her, she meant only to see if the roll top worked, but ended up opening it all the way and spying into a wonderful array of little cubbies, slots and tiny labeled drawers. One drawer read "bills," another "letters," and third "keys." Keys! She opened it ever so slightly and sure enough inside was a pile of silver and brass keys. House keys, car keys, padlock keys, suitcase keys, and yes, one big old-fashioned key which looked very much like it would fit into an old-fashioned keyhole.

Well, Katherine was a good girl, and certainly it would not be stealing, just to use something and then return it. Stealing, surely, is taking and NOT returning. Borrowing is taking AND returning. But just using... ? What do you think?

Nevertheless, Katherine did pick up the old key and waltzed nonchalantly up the two flights of stairs to the old crystal doorknob. To her glee it fit perfectly in the keyhole and the bolt turned easily out from the door jam. She cracked the door open an inch or two, shut it again, then quietly descended the stairs and returned the key to its drawer in the desk, which she rolled down to its original closed position. "There," she thought. "But why should an old lady living alone need a locked door anyway?"

Just then she almost leaped out of her skin as a bony hand caught her on the shoulder. "Why Katherine, dear, it's time to eat," said Aunt Clara gently, closing the door to the little room and ushering her niece into the dining room.

The next weekend Dad was away on business so we didn't come to Aunt Clara's, and the next weekend after that James was sick in bed with a fever. So it was a full three weeks before Katherine was again standing before that third floor door and wondering if it would still be unlocked. First she peered through the keyhole and the teacup was still on the floor, broken. But there was a tiny silver spoon lying next to it which she hadn't noticed before. At least she didn't think she'd noticed it before. Certainly she would have remembered if there was a spoon with the teacup or not. What do you think?

So she tried the door and it opened with a disturbing squeak. Spitting daintily on the hinges fixed that straight away and for the first time she was inside the third floor room. Actually it was more of an attic, but nicely furnished as a comfortable little room. The plaster walls were painted a pleasant green and there were thin yellow curtains at the single round window. In addition to the bed, the bureau and the rocker there was a small table with two chairs at it, and a steamer trunk. To her great relief there was no grandmother to be seen, alive or otherwise. But most wonderful of all, on the floor against the far side wall stood the most amazing dollhouse she had ever set eyes on. It looked like a grand Victorian mansion with four floors and eight tall chimneys. On top was a guard railed widow's walk and a tall ship weathervane.

There was real glass in the windows and tiny furniture in every room. She could clearly see the parlor, the study, the dining rooms, the kitchen, the bathrooms and into each bedroom. There were heavy miniature drapes at the windows and the beds were even made with thin little sheets. There was a miniature basin and pitcher for water on each washstand. Every window and door actually opened and she longed to open the back to begin play. Still, mindful of the time, she carefully closed the door of the room, scurried down the many stairs and was in her seat for dinner well ahead of us boys.

For one reason or another, several more weeks passed before she was again able to visit the third-floor room. This time she went straight to the dollhouse, intending to open its back and start rearranging furniture. Curiously the back did not open, and neither, she discovered, did the roof. "Now how is a girl to play with such a house?" she exclaimed half out loud. Nevertheless she contented herself with looking in the windows and opening and shutting the front and back doors. All too soon it was time to go, so she said farewell to her special mansion in which nobody lived but which had everything a person could ever want.

~4~
A Saturday Instead

L ike I've said before, we had always visited Aunt Clara on Sundays after church, but at this particular time our parents would be out of town all weekend, so we arrived bright and early on Saturday. After a very special blueberry pancake breakfast, which Katherine helped prepare, James and I headed out to the yard to seek our fortunes as a pirate and a big game warden respectively. As it turned out I spent most of my time protecting the local plants and animals from the pirate poachers in the area. We had coaxed Katherine outside for a while but she soon tired of being teased with snail slime, spider webs, and grasshopper tobacco juice.

"Kath, you're a sissy," James had said. "Frogs don't bite. Here, grab it by his hind legs."

"Eeiuu, get it out of my face," she squealed, "It's gooey. I'm not holding it. Anyway, I have something much more interesting to do in the house."

"What?" asked James, picking an iris to tickle the frog with.

"Oh, a dollhouse," she said, knowing full well that *that* information would be enough to keep us boys away.

"Okay, go play with your dolly-dolls," we said giving her good riddance, for she was so out of place in our jungle or army games, and tended to dampen our enthusiasm.

So it was just a little before nine A.M. that Katherine peered down again at the great doll house. As her eyes moved across the long row of upper windows she stopped at a curious sight. One of the beds in one of the bedrooms was unmade. Not just unmade, it was a complete wreck. The sheets and blankets were half on the floor and the pillows were there in the middle of the bed where they don't belong. Everything was mussed and unruly. "Strange," she reflected. "I don't remember a room being like this. Who could be playing in this house? Certainly Aunt Clara's hands would be too large to reach through this tiny window and make such a clutter. Why there are even flannel pajama bottoms left carelessly on the floor leading to the bathroom. Aunt Clara would never leave such untidiness. What could this be? Another girl must be playing here! But who? Well I should at least straighten up a bit."

So Katherine proceeded to open the tiny window and thrust two small fingers inside to deal with the mess if she could. At first only two fingers would fit, but then presently four, and then her whole hand would fit nicely inside the window. Mind you, the window never grew in size, it was as if her hand seemed to be shrinking.

Knowing this to be impossible, or at least, very dangerous, she quickly withdrew it and everything appeared normal again.

"How odd!" she exclaimed.

After a moment of meditation building up her courage, she tried it again with the same results. This time she got her whole arm inside and actually was able to straighten out the bed a little. When she withdrew her arm everything returned to normal again. Her freckled cheeks so pasty white at first, soon became flushed with excitement.

"So *this* is why the back doesn't open," she reflected, "it doesn't need to. This is a doll house you can reach into! How utterly mysterious and magical!"

She began to stick her arm in everywhere, moving this, rearranging that, until she came upon a lovely fur coat carelessly left on the floor of a closet. She was able to get it on a hanger alright, but it kept slipping off when she hung it up beside the other clothes.

"I need to button it first," she figured, but this proved to be highly frustrating with one hand. So in went her other hand, but then her face was outside against the roof, making it was impossible to see anything.

"Maybe, if I just duck my head in too," she thought, and so she did. "Yes, that's much better!" And before she knew it, she was leaning in the window all the way to her waist. Soon she spied a door on the far wall which she obviously couldn't reach without legs so she proceeded to summersault forward all the way through the window and completely into the house. Standing up inside she checked herself and apart from a slightly bruised knee, she was perfectly fine – except for the fact that she was now a mere three inches tall.

"Three inches tall! Well, I don't FEEL three inches tall," she said out loud, "but what if I'm trapped in here?"

So she thrust her arm back out the window and it became large again. In fact it became so large it flopped on the floor outside, pulling the rest of her out along with it.

She was now, all of her, normal size again. "Oh, how awkward," she cried, adjusting her skirt, "I'll need to learn how do this more gracefully."

Indeed, by lunchtime she had become quite well practiced in the art of entering and exiting the house, shrinking and growing, shrinking and growing. This, she discovered, was much more easily accomplished using the doors than the windows.

~5~
James Joins In

At the lunch table Katherine was positively popping with excitement over her discovery. Yet she certainly couldn't tell Aunt Clara because of the key thing and because of the fact that maybe she wasn't allowed upstairs at all. So after the last sandwich was consumed, the dishes were cleaned up and our Aunt was safely upstairs for her nap, Katherine broke her news.

"Guess what!" she bubbled, grabbing at my shirtsleeve, "there's a third floor to this house, with a room with a dollhouse, and the bed was unmade so I, well, it's true! I stuck my whole arm in and, and." She gasped for a breath, "*and* it went all the way in and so did my other arm and, and, and my other head and, and."

"Your other *head*?" roared James, shoving her aside.

"NO, my other LEG," barked Katherine, "ALL of me went into the dollhouse!"

I must admit I was less than gracious at hearing this fantastic tale, and was perhaps even a bit brutal as I joined James in scoffing and sniggering. Katherine, however, held her ground and stared at us with big condescending eyes. James finally ran away into the den but later tagged along after her in secret. I had gone outside, tired of such foolishness.

"Is there a basement where there might be skeletons?" James asked her at the bottom of the stairs. She ignored him, but took his hand to lead him up. He jerked it away, but Katherine's finger to her lips held him captive and quiet. She ushered him silently past Aunt Clara's bedroom, up the next flight of stairs and into the third floor chamber.

"There, you see, it's real. A mansion. Isn't it just super?" she purred, fingering the railing on the widows walk.

James spun the weathervane and almost broke it off. "This is a pirate ship," he announced, "the Black Cutlass."

"It's no such thing," countered Katherine, "the captain of that ship owns this house and his beautiful young wife from England waits weeping for him at this railing – every evening at sunset."

"Yeah, she's crying because my pirates have strung him up from the yardarm and sunk his ship. His gold is *ours*!"

Katherine slapped his arm away from the weathervane, "Stop, you're bending it."

Now there would come a time when James would be able to throw his big sister to the floor and give her a sound beating, which he sorely wanted to do now, but such a time would not come for a few years. Luckily by then James would outgrow his piratical instincts and he would even become a gentleman. I think *that* happened when he was about thirty-five.

This day, however, James could only glare back at his sister. It was a battle he would always lose. So he gazed instead like a cat, disinterestedly about the room and eventually into a dark and hitherto unnoticed corner. "Is that a castle?" he squealed.

Katherine had never noticed it before and had to admit it looked, in its own way just as imposing as the Victorian mansion. For one thing it had a moat and a drawbridge that really went up and down on a tiny chain. The walls were very thick and heavy with arrow-slit windows and battlements on top of them. Inside the courtyard stood a highly detailed miniature trebuchet for catapulting huge stones or burning embers at attackers.

An extremely tall, round tower with a gray cone roof of slate topped everything off. A queen could be held captive in such a tower, or a mad prince in chains.

"I want to play with it," James said immediately, as he reached to pry off the roof of the tower.

"Stop it! Be careful," warned Katherine, "wait, let's try something."

Sure enough, when she reached inside the dark mouth by the drawbridge her whole hand seemed to disappear.

James excitedly pulled it out and thrust his own inside all the way up to the armpit. "I can't feel anything," he said.

"Hold it," said Katherine, "put your head in too, so you can see where you're going."

"Won't it get stuck?" asked the little boy.

"No, here, see." She guided him gently all the way in and then, gathering her courage, followed in herself.

Suddenly the two small children were standing directly beneath the gaping teeth of a huge portcullis, an iron-bound wooden grating ready to slide down in slots in front of the mammoth gateway. Quickly they scampered further inside the gatehouse and for the first time in his life, James was more than happy to take his sister's hand.

22

~6~
Levancrieff

S o there they were, two very small children, three inches tall, all alone in a rather cold and dank gray rock fortress.

"Are you scared?" Katherine asked.

"Of course not," pretended James, for pirates never admit to fear.

"Should we go up or down, then?" for there were several narrow, circular stairwells leading out of the chamber. Two went up and one, ominously, down. "I don't think we'd better go down into the dungeon just yet," said Katherine.

James, peering down into the blackness, agreed.

So the children started up one of the staircases, the one with the brighter light at the top. It seemed as if the stairs had been drilled into solid rock but if you looked closely you could perceive the massive stone blocks from which the castle was erected. Each stone step was well worn in the middle from countless feet over the centuries. There was no railing and Katherine wanted to keep hold of James' hand but the way was so narrow as to make that impossible.

Soon they came out into a great hall with a massive stone fireplace dominating. You could actually walk into the fireplace, which the children did without ducking their heads, even seeing daylight up the chimney. Above the fireplace was this inscription in the stone:

Regnat populus
Ne humanus crede

The only furniture in the room was a thick oak table with eight sturdy chairs around it. There were knife cuts and gouges in the table. Even more interesting to James, however was the complete suit of armor hanging in one corner. It had a pointed helmet with visor and fancy plumes, chain mail, gauntlets, a metal chest plate, boots and everything. Beside it rested a massive two-edged greatsword which James could hardly lift. It was all of five feet long. Together they managed to heft it onto the table and began inspecting the jewels in it.

"Could these be real gems in the handle?" exclaimed Katherine.

"Swords don't have handles, they have hilts," came the reply.

"Well la-di-dah, your Majesty," I can call it a handle if I want. "I think these green stones are real emeralds."

Just then there came a rustling from behind and turning, the children froze in their footprints, speechless.

A giant, gray rat had crept up behind them and was staring with beady, black eyes. Actually, of course it wasn't really a giant rat, it was a normal-sized rat, it's just that the children were small. The rat twiddled its whiskers at them. James clung to his big sister then hid squarely behind her. The rat held out its paw as if offering her something. Indeed there *was* something, a small acorn. Katherine tried to stay calm and quiet but she was trembling horribly, petrified at the sight of those enormous, curved, yellow front teeth. The rat inched closer holding the acorn out to her. Slowly, closer. Inching, creeping – closer, closer. Suddenly there came a muffled voice from another room.

"Sherwoode, get away from it, I don't think it likes nuts. Look at its teeth. Maybe it's a meat-eater. Get out of there, but don't turn your back on it. Let's wait 'till your father gets home."

"Ma, I think they're friendly," replied Sherwoode, "in spite of their grotesque sunken eyes and hairless faces. I feel sorry for them. Maybe they're sick."

"Get out of there this instant, I think they bite. I don't like the way that one's staring at you. I don't think it wants your nut."

As the rodent was slowly backing off, Katherine did a surprising thing. She spoke to it.

"No wait," she said, her voice cracking.

This made the rat jump and scurry into a corner. "You can speak!" it said, turning its face toward them.

"Well, I'm supposed to," said Katherine, "but since when can rats talk?"

"Since my mommy taught me, that's when. Are you ill?" asked Sherwoode.

"Why no, I'm quite fine, thank you. Why do you ask? You aren't going to eat us, are you?"

"Of course not, how disgusting! We don't eat every strange thing we find around the place. Who knows where it's been or who's handled it. Are you hairless weasels or something?"

"Weasels? Gracious, no. We're people," said Katherine.

"People? You couldn't be people. *we* are people. You know, *folks*, and you're certainly not folks like us," said the rat.

"We certainly *are* people! A girl and a boy. People. Humans," insisted Katherine.

"Oh, *humans*. Humans aren't people. Wait, aren't you a bit small for humans? And besides humans consist mostly of feet."

James, bolder now that the rat hadn't attacked them, and not wanting to be left out of the conversation, jumped out from behind his sister and squealed, "We shrank to get in here, and we're *not* grotesque."

"Oh I suppose not – to your own selves anyway, where are your whiskers?"

"I'll have plenty of them later, you'll see. I'll have a great black beard, a steel hook for a hand, and a frightful black patch over my bad eye."

26

"Shut up James, don't provoke it. There may be others. Do you think we could scare it away with this sword?"

But James paid no attention to her and instead approached the rat now cowering in the corner. "Mister Rat, do you have a name?"

"My name is Sherwoode but my friends just call me Woodiekins."

"Woodiekins, are you a boy then?"

"I'm a buck, if that's what you mean. Okay, a young buck if you must know."

"I'm the pirate, Captain James Kidd."

"What, a pirate without whiskers? The only pirates without whiskers are girls. You're not a girl are you?"

"Heavens no," said James, "but *she* is – my kid-sister Katherine the fraidy-cat," James poked her in the ribs.

"Quit it," said Katherine, "Actually, I think we should be leaving."

"Do you live here?" James demanded of the rat.

"Well yes indeed, with my mother and father. Do you want to see my room?"

"Not today, I'm afraid," Katherine interjected, ushering James toward the stairwell.

"Oh but you'll come tomorrow, won't you?" asked Woodiekins, "I really have no one interesting to play with here, and there's the dungeon, the tower and all sorts of secret passageways."

"We'll see," said Katherine.

"That sometimes means yes," interpreted James.

"Well you'd better get back here soon," said Sherwoode, "before they lower the gate and raise the drawbridge. Did you know that a castle such as our Levancrieff is coming under siege all the time. Enemies are set on killing our bucks, carrying off our does and eating our food."

"If I come back can I pretend to be a knight?" asked James.

"You can more than pretend in here," said Sherwoode. "Girl," he continued, "did you know that the green stones in that sword there are emeralds, quite real, but inedible."

Katherine turned, walked over and looked again. She started to pick at one of them.

"Careful, girl, that sword is magic. Its name is Logokrataioo."

"You may call me Katherine, and him James. Is that rat-language? What does it mean?"

"It means 'power word,' girl, and the language is Ancient Greek, not Rat."

"Say, while you're translating things, what do the Greek words over the fireplace mean?" asked James.

"Not Greek, Latin. The sword is much older even than this castle. In fact, I'm told the sword is *eternal*. It has no beginning and no end," said Sherwoode.

"Oh stop!" said Katherine, "Only God is eternal. James, I think we should be going. Master Sherwoode, thank you for your hospitality."

"Girl, rats never lie," replied Sherwoode evenly.

"Why won't you say my name?" asked Katherine.

28

"No offence, girl," answered the rat, "but it's bad luck to use any name that begins with 'cat.'"

"But hers starts with 'Kath,'" James piped up.

"Same thing! Our front teeth are so big that 'th' sounds just like 't' to us," said Sherwoode.

"Fine, suit yourself," said Katherine, "but we really must be going."

With this, they started somewhat awkwardly down the stairwell. Soon, over their shoulders they heard Sherwoode calling after them. "Oh, girl and James, by the way, the fireplace says 'LET THE PEOPLE RULE, TRUST NO HUMAN.'"

Without replying, they picked up their pace, scrambled over the drawbridge and sprinted clear out of the castle, regaining their original size once again.

After catching their breaths, James noticed he was still holding his sister's hand. He dropped it immediately, giving her a look. They both brushed themselves off. It was getting late so they headed downstairs and were soon tucked safely into their beds for the night.

~7~
Mousumerset Manor

At first light and before anyone else in the house was awake, Katherine and James climbed the stairs to the third floor again. James headed directly for the castle, but Katherine caught his arm.

"We were lucky to get out of there yesterday," she exclaimed, "I don't trust rats, never have."

"What's so bad about rats?" demanded James, "I thought he was quite friendly."

"I don't like their tails."

"What's that got to do with anything?"

"They're ishy, that's all. And they're so big and disgusting. It seems rodents don't shrink when they go into the castle like we humans do. So lets go into the mansion instead."

"Kath, pirates don't go into dollhouses except for pillaging and I don't have a sword to pillage with. Let's go back into the castle and find one my size."

"You're not going in there alone, that's for sure, and besides, it's my turn to go into the mansion. So you must either come with me or just wait right here. Go take a nap in that bed or something. Better yet, clean up that broken teacup. Maybe you can find some glue and put it back together."

James made a face but did start poking around the room ostensibly in search of glue.

"Alright, I'll be back in a jiffy; you wait here," Katherine said as she entered the front door of the house.

James' eyes widened as he saw her shrink into the doorway and then walk into the grand entrance hall. He called in after her but she couldn't hear him. "I guess sound doesn't shrink like people do," he supposed.

Not finding any glue, (and why should he clean up the cup anyway, he didn't break it), he considered entering the castle again. He'd been brave enough in there with his sister at his side, but maybe there was something to her warning about the trustworthiness of rats. Certainly he *could* be in there alone but she had told him not to and, wait, he would go get William. William would surely love it in there; they could help each other over walls, have swordfights, and the rats would be afraid of William. He could brandish that greatsword at them. He'd go right now and get him.

And so he did, waking me up from a peaceful slumber, wherein I was rescuing a fair, helpless maiden from a fire-nostriled t-rex. My sword brandishing so astonished the monster that he fled without receiving so much as a scratch. The girl was so impressed that she flung herself about my neck compelling me to flee in fear of a possible kiss. Kisses are known to be venomous to boys, even older men, although the effects of the toxin vary with the age of the victim.

Meanwhile in the mansion, Katherine had come upon the dining room where the table was set for an elaborate dinner. At each of twelve places was a lovely china plate bracketed by three knives, three forks and four spoons. Each person was to have a huge white linen napkin and two ornate lead-crystal goblets.

Katherine wrinkled her nose at the butter knife at each place setting. "That's too many utensils," she reflected, and proceeded to collect up all the butter knives, save one which she placed on the oval butter dish in the middle of the table. "There, that's better," she muttered.

Just then she heard some scurrying and shushing and then squeaking, but in the unmistakable tone of – a rat.

"What's she doing to the table?" it said, "Mary's so particular about where everything should go and now she's just ruining it. Oh fuss and bother. Look, only one butter knife now for the whole table! How tacky, how unsanitary! Oh fuss. Oh bother."

"Hush Adeylia, you'll be overheard. How do we know she's as friendly as Mary?"

"She *looks* friendly."

"I know, but looks can be deceiving. See her teeth? She has no incisors. How hideous."

"How then does she eat?"

"She must still suck from a baby bottle. Their mothers won't even suckle their young."

"How repugnant, how plebian."

"How monstrous. Oh fuss."

"Excuse me, you rats, but I can hear you and you're hurting my feelings," said Katherine, peering around the corner at them.

"Rats! Oh but we're not *rats*," squealed Luucy, the larger of the two.

"Well yes," Katherine replied apologetically, "I can see that now. You're quite small and cute."

"Oh yes, cute I suppose, but don't call my husband cute. My daughter Adeylia is the cute one, don't you agree."

"Oh my yes, she's an adorable little mouse. Do you live here in this house?"

"Why certainly we do, but we come and go for food."

"What do you eat?" asked Katherine, gazing at the place settings on the table.

"Only cake," piped up Adeylia, "you don't happen to have any now, do you?"

"Oh, I'm sorry, I don't, but would you like me to bring some next time I come?"

"We do always seem to be short of cake," said Luucy.

"And shortcake!" said Adeylia.

"And shortbread!" added Luucy.

"Okay, I get the point – sweet teeth," said Katherine.

"Oh, it's not for us. We don't eat such things," said Luucy, "it gives us such sugar-highs. Adeylia gets hyperactive and Lesster downright agitated. Me, I've never eaten cake, so gracious knows what I would be like."

"I can scarcely believe that you mice never eat cake. Then who's it for?"

"Why Mary, silly," said Adeylia.

"Who is this Mary?"

"Why she's just a bigger version of you, my dear, but your fur has red highlights, and hers yellow," said Adeylia.

"Hair, darling," Luucy interjected.

"Oh that's right. I learned about hair in home school," said Adeylia, "but it's all fur to me. And Mary, at least has her two front teeth."

"Where is this Mary?" asked Katherine.

"She must be hiding," said Luucy, "Maybe she won't like you. You know what they say about 'having only one woman per household.' – Well, we mice don't say it, that would be impolite. Humans say it."

"No, we don't say any such thing. Will you take me to Mary? Is she home?" asked Katherine.

"Oh, she's home alright," replied Adeylia, "always. In fact it seems she can't leave Mousumerset. Not that she ever wants to. We bring her all the food she needs and she prepares it her way. It's no bother at all, she eats so little. She sleeps upstairs in a synthetic fluff nest called a bed. She doesn't speak English though, so you'd better not go up to see her."

"No English? Then what does she speak?"

"Mouse."

"Mouse? So where did YOU learn English?"

"Oh we don't speak English. We speak Mouse."

"But you're speaking English right now."

"Oh no, Mouse."

Katherine threw up her hands in despair, scaring the mice behind a door. "Oh, I'm sorry. But we *are* speaking English and I *am* going upstairs to find her. If you don't mind."

"Be careful, then," warned Luucy, "she's cranky in the morning. And *do* smooth out your hair a bit first. First impressions, you know."

"Would you call your hair more dishwater blond or mousy brown?" asked Adeylia.

Ignoring this with a stare, Katherine proceeded up three flights of stairs and went straight to the bedroom where she'd seen the unmade bed the other day. The mice followed along behind uneasily, making muffled comments every so often.

As they entered the room they found the bed neatly made but from the bathroom, there was a warm, steamy, strawberry feeling flowing in the air.

"Don't go in," warned Adeylia, "she might be in the bathtub."

Katherine walked over to the half-open door and tapped gently. "Hello? Mary? – Are you in there?"

"See, I told you she's not there in her bubble bath," said Luucy.

"Yeah, and she's not using the lavender soap we gave her for Christmas either," added Adeylia.

"Mary," called Katherine again, "I would so much like to meet you. I will wait for you downstairs. We'll have a nice breakfast waiting."

There was no answer, but Katherine saw a pink soap bubble or two blow out the bathroom door as they turned to leave the bedroom. Nicely framed at the side of the door Katherine spied a list of rules elegantly penned in copperplate handwriting with beautiful broad S-shaped downstrokes and light, thin upstrokes.

Mary's Ten Rules of
Manners (making the other person feel at ease)
and
Etiquette (a collection of specific manners)[1]

1. Hand motions should lead with the wrist.

2. A dinner napkin should be unfolded to half its size (luncheon napkin full size); a lady's napkin goes on lap, and a man's napkin goes on right leg.

3. Serve food from left, remove used plates from right.

4. A beverage served in a large goblet should be picked up by the thumb and two fingers around the base of the bowl, never the stem.

5. Break off rolls and butter it a piece at a time; if a salad plate is provided it should hold bread or rolls, butter and salad.

6. If you must put them into soup, crackers or croutons must be put in whole, not crumbled.

7. Gravy should be poured on, or beside, the meat. With your fork dip potato into gravy.

8. When holding a cup, never extend or bend the little finger; this gives an affected look.

9. Eating cake: any cake that is sticky should be eaten with a fork; pound cake (ungarnished) is eaten with the fingers; filled éclairs should be eaten with a fork. Always leave some crumbs on the table for the ants.

10. How to leave a room: walk to door, open it, then look back over your shoulder (or turn) and smile, then leave. Don't slam the door.

"Okay, you two go down and cook something nice," broke in Luucy, "that is, if we're going to surprise Mary with such a late breakfast. I'll go out, get some fresh fruit and collect my Lesster."

"See, I told you," said Adeylia as they entered the kitchen.

"Told me what?" asked Katherine.

"Oh nothing, if you don't already know, you never will. Shall we make Poached Eggs Florentine?" suggested Adeylia.

"I don't exactly know how, but I'm pretty good at flapjacks," Katherine shrugged.

"FlapWHAT? – Not pancakes! We're not serving a lumberjack, you know."

"Okay, okay then, where are the eggs?"

"Why in the egg basket, silly. But I can't crack them, I'm all thumbs, mind you. You'll have to do that."

"And a pan to poach them in?"

"No, Mary just fries them on the griddle here." replied Adeylia.

"Oh, so they're fried, not poached," said Katherine.

"Uh, duh! I said *poached* Eggs Florentine. So we poach them from the henhouse next-door, *fry* them and serve them on a nice bed of flowers."

"Hmm," replied Katherine, "I may not know everything but I believe 'Florentine' indicates spinach."

"Spinach! You're right, you don't know everything. Spinach's not a breakfast food."

"But I don't eat flowers!"

"Well, Mary does! And eats them with relish."

After a considerable amount of time fussing about and not getting much done toward breakfast, Katherine decided it was getting late and James would be wondering what happened to her. "Well, Adeylia, it's been fun, but I really must go and see how my brother's doing."

"But you'll come back soon, won't you?"

"Yes, of course, and may I see your room next time?" asked Katherine.

"Oh sure, but be sure to wipe your feet and don't touch anything fragile."

"Bye then," replied Katherine, rolling her eyes.

~8~
I Get Involved

When Katherine left Mousumerset Manor, James was nowhere to be seen. She walked over to Levancrieff Castle. She peered into the windows but saw only empty rooms. Even the rats seemed to be gone. Of course they could all be in the dungeon torturing her brother, but she put such thoughts out of her head, preferring to think instead that he'd simply tired of the game and left the third floor altogether.

Thoughts of Poached Eggs Florentine made her realize that she was hungry so she headed down the stairs to Aunt Clara's kitchen. Sometimes there was a sticky bun to snitch or something else left out on purpose, even between meals. There was.

James, of course was not in the kitchen, he was upstairs waking me out of the dream in which I was fleeing down the steps of a castle. "Oh but you NEED to come," he said, "there's this toy castle to play in."

At first I was not at all sure that I wanted to return to a castle, real or not. "Are there plastic knights and damsels?" I asked.

"What are damsels?"

"Damsels are helpless young girls that need to be rescued from dragons."

"Why?"

"Dragons like to eat them. No, wait. I think they'd rather keep them as pets."

"Whatever for? Anyway there were no girls or dragons in the castle, just a rat named Sherwoode," said James.

"Sherwoode? Did you make up that name?"

"No, it's his real name, but they call him Woodiekins for short."

"That's funny," I said, "Woodiekins isn't shorter than Sherwoode."

"Never mind – to the rats it is," insisted James, "are you going to come and see him?"

Now I was intrigued at the idea of seeing a rat, and there might even be a kernel of truth in what James was saying. Of course rats don't talk and they certainly don't give each other names. Still, I was wide awake now, so I trundled behind my little brother all the way up to the third floor landing.

"I don't think we should go any further," I said, "who said you could be up on the third floor anyway? We're not allowed."

"Katherine's up here in a dollhouse."

I assumed he meant *playing* in a doll house. "Okay, lets go get her and we'll all go down and ask Aunt Clara if we can play up on the third floor."

So we two boys carefully opened the door and immediately spied the Victorian Mansion.

"There's the dollhouse," I said, "but no Katherine."

"No, I said she was *in* the dollhouse," replied James.

"Okay, dim-wit," I said, somewhat irritated, "lets look in the windows – see, she's nowhere to be found. My, this dollhouse certainly is realistic, though. There's even food on the table here."

"Okay, William, but look, the castle's over here in the corner," said James, tugging at my shirt, "I'll show you how we get in."

We went over to the castle. I was puzzled at James' behavior. "Stop trying to stick your whole arm into it. It's a toy, you'll break it,." I said.

"No, I got into it this way before," pleaded James, getting more and more frustrated.

"Okay dude, I'm sure you did, so where's this rat you were talking about?"

"INSIDE."

"Well it doesn't seem to be in there now," I scoffed.

"Okay, okay, it sometimes goes out for food. You wait here, I'm going to get Katherine, she'll tell you. She must have gone downstairs for something. You wait. I'll be right back."

With this, and after another quick glance into the dollhouse, James swept out of the room and silently down the stairs. I sat quietly in front of the castle noticing the intricate detail of its construction. It seemed to be made of real stone and not painted plastic or wood. Suddenly in the corner of my eye it seemed like there was movement in the dollhouse across the room. There it was again and then, unmistakably the drawing of a curtain across an upstairs window.

A tingling sensation rushed down my spine and settled in my stomach. Maybe there *were* rats in the houses? But would a rat draw a curtain? Slowly I crept over, quietly opened the glass window and drew back the curtain. To my amazement I saw a tiny girl-doll inside. She was wearing a pink bathrobe. Her light-brown hair was long, wet, curly – messy. Her eyes had an elfin sparkle and there were freckles on her little nose and cheeks, but not too many. She had an impish smile. I was amazed at how realistic this doll was and thought it looked quite like some of the girls in my class at school. I suppose my mouth hung open a bit as I peered more closely in the window.

Impossibly, the doll's eyes seemed to open wider and peer curiously back into my own. Suddenly a tiny hand reached up to cover a tiny mouth, and bending over to pick up a wet towel, she made a hasty retreat into the bathroom. I tried to peer in after her but to no avail, she had scurried into parts unknown. I even tried to cram my fingers in the window but they didn't fit.

Shaken, I just sat against the far wall, and tried to figure things out rationally. But the more I thought, the more confused I got because logic simply doesn't apply to dollhouses. Or to girl-dolls. Or to girls for that matter. Finally I headed back down the stairs.

~9~
Salvation Explained

Katherine was surprised to pass her big brother on the steps leading to the second floor. "Oh William," she said, "by the way, have you seen James? I seem to have lost him."

"He's looking for you too," I replied. "He's not upstairs."

With a shrug, Katherine turned to continue her ascent, but then asked over her shoulder, "Say, what were you doing up there?"

"Oh, he was showing me some dollhouses up on the third floor. Are we allowed up there?"

"William, you won't tell, will you? I found a key to the door and…"

"We should lock that place up again and forget all about it. I just saw a doll up there move, all by itself."

"Did she talk to you?"

"Talk?" then after a pause, "No, she ran away and hid."

"Did you go in after her? I don't think we can hear through the windows."

"What? You're crazy. I poked my fingers in and they almost got stuck. I couldn't get in even if I wanted to. It's retarded, playing with dolls anyway. I'm going back outside. I think you should lock that door and stay away. It's ridiculous."

With that, I sped down the stairs and headed out into the yard. But just beyond the screen door I was collared by Aunt Clara's long, bony arm.

"Everybody, quick grab a sticky bun and bundle into the car. We're running late for church," she squawked.

I was able to waylay Katherine still on the stairs and catch James in the kitchen swallowing a whole chocolate éclair in snakelike fashion.

We made it to church just in time for either the very front pew or the very back. Of course our aunt, proud to exhibit us children, chose the front and plunked us down right in the center. She sat between the two youngest and surreptitiously gave James a hard candy and a coloring book. During the hymns when Katherine wouldn't share my hymnal, Aunt Clara actually pinched her hard on the arm. Katherine kept inspecting the site as if expecting blood or at least a bruise.

The sermon, when it finally came was aptly entitled, "Salvation, Is It Kids' Stuff?" I found the subject engaging since it addressed the issue of children being saved. James was too occupied with coloring his dinosaur to be concerned. Katherine, on the other hand, was too old for coloring books but too young to catch the subtle issues being presented. So, soon she was fidgeting with her fingers, then with her hair, then with the buttons on her dress. I poked her once or twice, only to get a look, and then a mean stare. Finally when I persevered, she lowered her eyebrows ominously and essentially stuck out her tongue at me. It was one of those pouty-lipped partly-protuberant tongue things that girls do. Disgusting. Most of the stinging message, however is carried in the eyes and the thrusting of the chin. Aunt Clara caught a glimpse of this and immediately, awkwardly and in front of the whole congregation, moved over between us. This I found humiliating and insulting. Across our Aunt's ample lap, Katherine kept glancing at me with a smug look. She assumed that I, being older, was the one who had fallen the farther from grace.

At dinner we were both models of propriety but after the dishes I grabbed Katherine's arm, roughly pulled her into the little den, and closed the door firmly behind us.

"Hey, you're hurting my arm!" she said, sticking out her chin, "go ahead and hit me, I'm not afraid of you. I hope you leave a mark." She was a brave little thing, I had to give her that.

"I don't hit girls," I said, "I just want to know why you were so squirmy in church. It's a bad example for James."

"I dunno," she replied, "I guess I just didn't like the sermon."

"Why?" I said, "It was about children."

"Children?" she exploded, "I didn't hear anything about children."

"What?" I replied, "are you missing your frontal lobe as well as your front teeth?"

"My what?"

"Your brain, dim-wit, are you missing your brain?"

Her face started to fall and I knew I'd pressed her too hard. "Alright, sorry, Katherine. Didn't you understand the sermon? – Is that it?"

"Okay, okay, I didn't get it! I'm not in high school, you know, but I'm not stupid."

"Do you want me to tell you what the sermon said?" I asked.

"Well if you insist," came the reply. "If you'd done that in the first place we wouldn't be having all this trouble."

Biting back a smart remark, I pulled her down next to me on the loveseat and began. "The sermon was explaining how kids can get saved," I said. She pivoted around on the seat cushion, hung her bare legs over the armrest, and rested her head in my lap.

Just then there was a knock at the door and James' piercing voice penetrated the woodwork, "Hullo's anybody in there? Can I come in?"

"NO!" we both bellowed in unison, and Katherine giggled and grabbed my hand in both of hers. This was our special time. After a few moments of silence, she closed her eyes and purred, "So how *do* kids get saved?"

"Well," I began, "God originally created people with the freedom to be friends with Him if they so choose. And to love Him and to tell Him how neat He is. But the first man, Adam disobeyed God. Because of that, all people are now born to rebel against Him. And they do."

"I know, Adam ate the apple which God told him not to," said Katherine excitedly.

"That's right," I said, "and naturally, God can't live with people who disrespect Him like that. So, since they'll never come back to Him of their own, He sent His Son to become a man."

"Jesus! But why? To rescue us?" asked Katherine.

"Yes, Jesus suffered the separation from God that all of us deserve. That's called 'death.'"

"On the cross," said Katherine.

"See you know this stuff," I smiled down into her face. "Jesus took our punishment, once and for all."

"Okay, but if Jesus was separated from God, then how did he get back up there in heaven with Him?

"Remember, Katherine, that Jesus Himself never rejected His Father. And, even though He's a man, He's also God. So with that strength and authority God smashed the power separating Jesus from His Father.

"Is that his resurrection from the dead?" asked Katherine.

"Exactly, but that does us no good if we don't individually accept Him as our King and join His Kingdom. Otherwise we're still lost. That's what it means to accept Jesus."

"Yeah, I get that, but I thought you said the sermon was about kids."

"It was," I continued, "so what do you think happens to little children who aren't old enough to understand about accepting Jesus as their King?"

"What, like James? Well they go to hell with the other brats."

So I asked her, "Do you really think that our God would send little babies into hellfire before they can even understand about believing in Jesus? Before they reach an age where they are responsible for their actions?"

"Oh I suppose not; can I leave now?" asked Katherine, dropping my hand and raising her head off my lap. I'm not sure she even knew what responsibility meant.

"Have you asked Jesus to be your King?" I queried bluntly.

"That's none of your beeswax," came the reply and the special moment dissolved as quickly as it had begun. Katherine swiveled off the couch, straightened her dress and bolted from the room in pixie-girl fashion, banging the door behind her.

My sister and I would never again have a conversation about her salvation, but that very evening would find me talking to another girl, on another loveseat, on the same topic, yet with very different results.

But I'm getting ahead of my story.

~10~
James Gets an Explanation

After James was denied entrance to the den he headed upstairs in a huff. He'd show us. He didn't need us anyway. He could go into that castle all by himself if he wanted to. Why maybe he'd even find a sword and bring it out with him. Maybe he'd even smash a few windows in Katherine's precious dollhouse. Well he could do that if he wanted to, couldn't he?

This brash enthusiasm became tainted a bit as he again stood within the cavernous mouth of the castle drawbridge. Suddenly he felt frighteningly small, with a queasy sensation in his belly. Slowly, tentatively he climbed his way back up into the great hall.

"Woodiekins?" he called out in a thin voice, but there was no reply. The room was exactly as they had left it. Even the greatsword Logokrataioo was still lying on the floor. An ant was running purposefully down the middle of its shiny, sharp blade. James bent down to swat it away but thought twice since it was, upon closer inspection, the size of a lobster. Not only that, but as he approached, the ant addressed him in a hollow, gravelly voice.

"Excuse me, sir, but please pick up your sword. It's blocking our ant-trail and our thankless workers have enough to do cleaning up after your crumbs and refuse – without having to crawl over this silly spear thing every time."

"You talk!" gawked James in reply.

"Yes we TALK, but apparently you people don't LISTEN. Stop dropping crumbs everywhere. Stop spilling your food. It's getting tedious to venture out on dangerous floors to clean up after you. You *know* this. We've told you before."

"But I didn't drop crumbs! I'm new here. Maybe it's the rats."

"What, you're not a rat? Oh, oh yes I see now," said the ant, inspecting James a bit closer through his black, goggle-like eyes. "I suppose not. But you're all the same nevertheless. NON-ant, and therefore messy, unproductive and disgustingly wasteful."

"Do you have a name?" asked James, trying to change the subject.

"The Sixty-seventh Myleswalker of the Three-hundred Eightieth Brigade, Fifty-thousandth Regiment, Junior the Third is the name I commonly go by, but you can just call me Junior the Third for short. Not that you'll ever see me again, and if you should, not that you'd recognize me."

"I think I'll just call you Myles," said James, "I'm sorry but I'm too small to lift that sword out of your way. Would you like me to try and drag it over into the corner?"

"That would be the least you could do, I suppose."

So James sat down and shoved the sword across the floor with his feet. It was not an easy task and he got a big splinter in his bottom for his troubles. "Oh, by the way," he asked when he was finished and dusting himself off, "I'm looking for Woodiekins the rat. Do you know where he might be?"

"A rat? Well it might be playing in the mud in the moat. It might be spreading cake crumbs all over the kitchen floor. It might be taking swordfight or etiquette lessons to impress – only the bat knows who – or why. But I think you'll find it tearing up a perfectly good lady's scarf to line its laziness nap-nest. And why on El's great globe would you want to associate with a rat anyway?"

"Never mind, is he upstairs then?"

"Just follow those stairs up, if you must."

"Will I see you here on my way down again?"

"Oh I sincerely hope not – but maybe" blurted the ant, and he continued upon his business self-importantly, swaggering into a crack in the wooden floor.

Now going further *up* was not what James had envisioned for his first adventure alone in the castle. Still, the ant might be watching and so as not to appear cowardly James headed up the narrow stone-carved steps. They were steep, circling up and up, around and around and then became narrower and narrower. There was no handrail and the stone-stairs under the boy's feet were worn alabaster smooth through countless years of ascending or descending feet. One slip and there would be a bumpy and painful slide back down the stone spiral. Finally reaching top he came out into a tiny round room with a crude wooden floor and a timber beamed ceiling. There were slit windows spaced at even intervals which let in air and light. In one corner was a heap of straw garnished with strips of colorful fabric and a bird feather or two. Sleeping soundly on this nest, James spied Woodiekins, his long, bare tail trailing out haphazardly onto the rough floor.

Now not knowing quite how to wake a sleeping rodent, and a snoring one at that, James gave a little tug at its tail. The snore stopped short with a little snort but still the rat slept. James pulled again with the same results. Then a third time. In fact every time he yanked the tail he would get a snort. Finally he grabbed the thing and attempted to pull the rat clear off its nest. With this Woodiekins let out a very long snort which continued until the boy let go of the tail. But still the rat slept. About this time James got suspicious so he just tapped the tail ever so lightly with his finger. Out came a short snort. Ah ha! Tap. Snort. Tap. Snort.

Finally tiring of the game James yelled into the rat's ear, "SNAKE!"

Woodiekins jumped high into the air, bumping James' nose on the way up, landed on his feet and scurried to his dresser to retrieve his fighting sword. "Ready for battle at all times!" he shouted.

"Yeah, right," said James, "except during nap time, I see."

"I was just pretending to be asleep," said Woodiekins.

"Hey," said James, his eyes glancing down, "that's a neat sword in your hand! Can I see it?"

"Sure," replied Woodiekins, offering it to him, blade first.

"You know," said James, fingering the razor like edge, "your *be ready for battle* motto is from our Pirate Code of Honor."

"Pirate Code?" said Woodiekins, "that sounds like a contradiction in terms. Pirates don't have any honor to codify."

"Oh yes they do," replied James, "they are honorable to their own pirate band. Here, see. I have a little plastic card with a skull and crossbones on one side and the Code on the other.

The Pirate Code [2]

1. Obey the captain.
2. The captain receives a double share of all spoils.
3. Be ready for battle at all times.
4. You will be compensated for an amputation.
5. Do not desert the company.
6. Do not steal from the company.
7. Keep no secrets from the company.
8. Do not strike another man in the company.
9. Never carry an open flame in the hold of the ship or smoke in bed.

10. Do not molest a woman in public without her consent or smuggle one on board.

"And all Pirates carry these?" inquired the rat.

"Ever since ancient times," said the boy.

"How handy they're drivers license size. Easy for carrying in pirate wallets, or using to cash checks in grocery stores."

"Stop making fun of it. At least we pirates have a set of rules to live by."

"Oh, really? I have a better set of rules for you. They're more ancient than yours and frankly make more sense. Pirates, for instance have only a narrow concept of loyalty. Ultimately they are beholden only unto themselves. And their attitude towards honorable women is no better than shameful."

Well," admitted James, "to tell you the truth, I suppose I'm not really all that committed to the pirates and I'm certainly not all that thrilled about girls either."

"Oh, that'll change in time, my friend," said Woodiekins, "the girls part, I mean, mark my words. Would you like to hear the Code we go by in this castle?"

"Sure."

So Woodiekins began reciting from memory:

The Ten Commandments of Chivalry [3]

1. Serve and defend your heavenly El and earthly king.
2. Administer justice.

3. Protect the weak and innocent.

4. Fight evil in all its forms.

5. Never attack the unarmed, or from behind.

6. Never abandon a comrade, a just cause, or your principles.

7. Always keep your word of honor and your sword honed.

8. Obey the commands of ladies in the service of Love.

9. Do not love any woman you would be ashamed to marry.

10. In practicing the solaces of love never exceed the desires of your lover.

"If I do all this can I become a knight?" begged James, without having even the faintest idea what solaces might be.

"Have you reached the age of true accountability?" inquired the rat.

"The what age?"

"The age at which you're able to choose between loyalty to El and king or loyalty elsewhere."

"Oh I'm old enough for that," James assured him..

"I think not," demanded the rat, "show me your teeth."

"What's teeth got to do with it?" snapped James.

"Why everything!" said the rat, "see, you still have your baby teeth! Look at your upper central incisors. Without adult teeth you're not an adult. It's as simple as that. See how nice and big mine are?"

"Oh that's ridiculous," cried James.

"How do you think you're able to get inside this castle? It's because you're still a child," said Woodiekins.

James did note a ring of truth in this because William had not been able to enter the castle. "Hey wait," he said, "how come Katherine could get in, she's lost her baby front teeth.

"Oh, but very soon, when the first upper central incisor erupts from her gums, she'll be an accountable adult. You had better warn her of that," said Woodiekins imposingly.

"Warn her of what?"

"Of the Incise Enchantment," said the rat. "Of the fact that when her first front tooth appears she'll no longer be able to shrink into the castle. OR GO OUT, if she's trapped inside at the time."

"So *that's* what's behind the magic!" said James, "I'd better tell her, for sure. But I guess it can wait, since she's not in here now. Meanwhile will you show me how to use this sword properly? All the pirates I know just hack and poke around haphazardly."

"Well, to begin with," said Woodiekins, "you should never hack, you should cut or slice. And you should never poke, you should thrust, but only at the right precise moments. Be ever mindful of your guard and be ready to parry. Never underestimate your adversary. It takes time to master the art of skillful swordsmanship."

"Are you taking lessons? Can I take them too?" bubbled James.

"Yes on both counts, my friend," said Woodiekins with his best rat smile.

"Then can I become a knight?"

"When you have the proper teeth and have properly matured your body, your mind and your honor, then most certainly you can become a Knight of Levancrieff. But are you willing to stay, and stay the course. Do the work? Render the sacrifices? Reap the rewards?"

"Oh yes! Please! Why should I ever want to leave?" implored James.

"Well, there's one thing, perhaps you could do," said the rat. "Don't you think the cute little maiden Katherine would also enjoy life in a castle? There certainly's a scarcity of cuteness amidst all these gray stones and gray rats, and besides there's no one to cook delicious dinners for us. We're literally living out of trash cans at the moment."

"I could ask her," replied James, "would she become a princess or something?"

"Oh, at least a queen," returned the rat, stretching his lips as best he could towards his pointed ears. This was difficult for him, for everyone knows how hard it is for a rat to smile effectively.

With this news, James sped off and down the winding staircase in search of his big and apparently cute sister, although about this, he often wondered.

But just as he was about to scoot through the drawbridge Myles the ant waylaid him and waved him into a dark corner of the gatehouse.

"What?" snapped James, "I'm in a hurry."

"Always a hurry – you people. You're just mindlessly spinning in exercise wheels, you know. Faster, faster, faster – but folly."

"Do you have a point to make," said James somewhat irritated, "I need to talk with my sister."

"That's exactly what I want to chat with you about. A comrade of mine heard you talking to the smelly rat in the tower."

"So what?" replied James, who figured there'd be ant spies everywhere.

"So the rat is *wrong* about how you and your sister get in here," returned Myles. Then he nodded his head and his antennae waved up and down pompously.

"So how *do* we get in then," said James, "tell me your version."

"Well, the truth has nothing to do with teeth, but everything to do with the fact that children are experts at wishing and believing. And adults are *not*."

"What do you mean?"

"I mean like when you wish upon a star all your dreams will come true. And if you just believe that you can fly over the rooftops and stay young forever, then you can do it. You really really can. Like magic. Of course you have to wish very very hard. Only children can wish and believe like that, and if *enough* children wish and believe for the same thing – why then all things are possible. Isn't that wonderful? Look at all the things that ants have achieved by acting in unison as a community."

James had to agree that it did sound rather marvelous, powerful even. And much easier and less dangerous than the way pirates got things done. He would have to try out this wishing and believing technique sometime.

With this, the ant cocked his head, saluted James and marched back into the core of the castle to rejoin his comrades and his queen.

~11~
A New Friend

After the encounter in the den, and while James was in the castle, Katherine meandered haphazardly around her Aunt's house, running her fingers over the furniture and thinking about things. She looked out the window at some dainty butterflies billowing cloudlike in the yard. They seemed so beautiful and free as they flittered about and filtered the sun. How unlike the quixotic rats and obsessive-compulsive mice of the dollhouses. Such butterflies are unfettered by codes of conduct or strict rules of etiquette. They are unconcerned about current events, trusting only in the simple instincts provided by their Creator.

Then she thought about what William had said about the claims of Christ on her heart. Did she really love Him? Did she really love anybody? Could she? Did she even know what love meant? She half wanted to make Christ her King like William was saying, but how could she do that if she wasn't even a princess? Surely He would accept no less. Why she wasn't even a princess's maid servant. Why she was little more than a waif when it came to the things of God. How could He accept her?

Finally Aunt Clara went down for her nap so she made straight for the Victorian Mansion and once inside started searching for the little doll I'd described, whom she assumed was Mary.

"Whoever this Mary is," she thought, "she's expert at hiding. Maybe she's in some secret passageway. I bet the mice could help me."

But there were no mice to be found at this hour of the day. Mice, as is their habit, usually sleep well into the late afternoon. Katherine did perceive a tiny face poking around a door, however. She stared as it kept popping in and out of view.

"I see you, funnyface," she finally said, not quite knowing what to expect since the creature looked, disturbingly, very much like a cockroach. Even so, it was oddly handsome, like a man in a brown waistcoat wearing a beret with two thin feathers sticking out. It had six spindly legs, four for walking, one presumably for holding a map or flashlight, and one, she supposed, for sporting an umbrella or parasol, depending on the weather. Would it have a sense of humor? What do you think?

"Funnyface!" it said, still not showing itself. "It's not your place, to call me a name. It brings me shame."

"Oh, I'm sorry to hurt your feelings, sir. You have a very nice face, really. Do you also have a name?"

"My name is Prunellla, and I'm a girl, not a fella."

"I'm a girl too!" exclaimed Katherine, "you don't bite, do you?"

"I was going to ask the same thing. Do you bite, pinch or sting?"

"Heavens no," cried Katherine.

"But you do, well, scowl, don't you?" said Prunellla, crawling from behind the door, "and growl. Oh, I'm sure you do!"

Katherine gasped and winced at the sight of a cockroach almost half her size, even if it *did* look like a man in a waistcoat.

"See, see I was right. You think I'm a sight."

"No, no, I'm just not – I mean I'm used to the little nasty things that creep and crawl all about our house leaving germs and roach droppings."

"What kind of droppings would you expect us to leave, or should we bundle them home? Would you believe?"

"You're funny," said Katherine. "Actually, I was looking for Adeylia the mouse, have you seen her?"

"A mouse?" shrieked Prunellla, "we never actually *see* them. Mice. Or talk to them. They're so picky and ditsy. We just *peer* at them from hiding places. They have hideous, hairy faces. At least *you* are clean and smooth."

"Well then," replied Katherine, "where have you *peered* at her recently? She said she'd help me find Mary."

"Who? Hairy Mary? She's trapped in here, you know."

"Yes her!" cried Katherine. "Where is she? Why's she trapped in here?"

"Why she's trapped here because of the Body-hair Curse, of course," said Prunellla seriously. "It states that no human with body-hair can enter or leave this house. That's because body-hair is basically bad and disgusting. See how clean and smooth I am."

Katherine did note a ring of truth to this. All the women she knew hated body hair, even to the point of shaving it off regularly. But a Body-hair Curse? Well it was true that William had not been able to enter the mansion, but the much younger James could. Except for the top of his head, James had no more hair than a tennis ball. "Hey wait," she said, "then how come mice get in? Except for their tails, they're all about body-hair."

"But they don't *shrink*, do they! See? – But they do stink!" added Prunellla.

"So where is Mary?" Katherine inquired a second time.

"Bat knows!" replied Prunellla.

"Who?"

"Oh that's just an expression. Our Monsignor Bat, who lives in the attic knows everyone and everything."

"The attic? May I go see him then?"

"Oh heavens no, there are spiders guarding the way up there and no roach has ever returned from there alive."

"I'm not afraid of spiders," Katherine pretended.

"Well if you want to be headstrong about it, then I can show you where the stairs are; they're not far."

"Thank you Prunellla. You're so kind."

"You are most welcome and fair," replied the roach politely, "I so enjoy talking to someone without facial hair."

~12~
Getting Up to Bat

The stairs leading up to the attic were narrow, dark and dirty. At least there was a railing of sorts for Katherine to cling at, but her small, white hand didn't trust it entirely. In her other hand she gripped a single, lit candle. Each step creaked and groaned in protest. Her thin, unsure legs wobbled a bit on them and she bowed her head as a dusty cobweb or two graced her hair and tickled her ears. The candle flame ignited part of the web and it briefly flashed and died, leaving only an acrid smoky smell. Katherine shuddered, wondering if she was catching the house on fire, but was afraid to look up to find out.

Presently, she pressed on and soon was standing in a little room at the top of the stairs. The room was actually a tiny hall with only one door at the end of it. On the walls of the hall were framed pictures of all sorts and sizes. And upon closer inspection, on each picture frame could be seen a shiny, black spider. Each had fabulously long, toothpick legs and a grapelike body. As Katherine approached, each cowered slowly behind its picture frame, but kept two or three bug eyes out to inspect her.

It was dark at the top of the stairs and the tiny candle afforded only enough light to vaguely discern the picture frames and a big round door handle. It did, however cast a penetrating, yellow eye-shine, reflected from each spider eye right back into Katherine's horrified gaze. She completely froze in place, speechless and unable to move one way or the other. Finally, in desperation, she started inching her way backwards down the first step and then the second. As her toe hit the third the awful silence was broken by a sweet, tiny voice.

"Hail girly. Oh, please don'ts s'go."

Katherine froze halfway between steps.

"Oh, please don'st s'go," the voice came again.

"I have a candle," said Katherine.

"We's know," answered the voice, "please don'st be s'afraid. We's don'st suck little girlys. Please don'st burn us'es. We's saying we's no one to talk to up here but ourselveses, and we's're bored silly with eachy other."

"Actually, I just came up here to talk to Monsignor Bat," said Katherine, alighting tentatively on the first step again.

"Moss Bat?" said the closest spider, "Silly s'bat. He's full of grasshoppers and they go to his head. Don't talk to him, talk to us'es. We're's more interestings."

"Oh, I'm sure you're fascinating, but I have business with the bat," replied Katherine.

"Oh bothersome businesses. Gives us all sick headaches. Swede s'rather be's sitting in webs of our own making than meddlin' in other's businesses."

Katherine shuffled forward toward the door, holding the candle high, and put her free hand firmly on the knob.

At this point a tinier, even more pleasing spider-voice piped up, "Oh pleasing, sweet, you'll please come back soon and speak with us all day about how to being a pretty girl like you. Why, I'm so hideous I wants't to cry. Who made you into a lovable lass and me into an unsightly spider? What sin of mine makes me so black and you so white? What did I do to deserve all these too many legs?" With this the baby spider began to sob. All her big sisters, cousins and aunts shot her disapproving looks but her mother gathered her in protectively under one of eight legs.

"What's your name, poor thing?" asked Katherine, not knowing quite what to say.

"Shcandelaria," replied the baby spider, clinging to her mother's hairy leg for reassurance. "Why thank you, nobody ever asks us'us our names."

"And oh," added her mother, "please lets a fly or two in before you close the door. Have a heart. Give a thoughts or twos for us poor spiders here. This place sucks."

~13~
The Bat Reveals the Truth

Katherine shuddered as she quickly, silently slipped through the door and closed it firmly and thankfully behind her. She pulled the cobwebs from her hair and smoothed out her dress. The attic was much brighter than the hall had been and her eyes squinted at the sunrays pouring through the window. She used her hand as a visor and soon was able to make out what looked like an old rat hanging by its tail from the low ceiling.

"My, my," it said, preening its patchy fur, "that's the hard way to get up here, certainly, indeed. Most of my friends use the front stairs to the widow's walk and then the narrow roof ledge and into this window. Oh, but I see, you've got a dress on and wouldn't want to ungracefully clamor into this tiny orifice, or muss your nice hair."

"Are you Monsignor Bat?" inquired Katherine squinting her eyes at him and wrinkling her nose a bit.

"Monsignor? Oh what nonsense. Who called me that? I'm not Monsignor, I'm just plain old Mister Bat. But since you're a human, you may call me by my given name."

When the bat didn't reveal what that name might be, Katherine asked.

"Oh it's too complicated for rodents and insects to understand," replied the bat.

"But I'm *not*... I'm a *human*," Katherine protested.

"Well I can *see* that, young lady. I can see that you're a human. And a rather impatient one too," said the bat.

Katherine just rolled her eyes and sat down in an old rocking chair that happened to be close by. She noticed the many old and dusty things about, including an old doll house not unlike the one she was in. She reflected on what might happen if she tried to enter *that* one as well. How tall would she be *then*? Still the bat said nothing, so she cocked her head at it. Still the bat said nothing.

Katherine cocked her head again. Finally in desperation she blurted, "Well, I..."

"I," said the bat at the same instant.

"Excuse me?" said Katherine.

"Okay," said the bat.

"Excuse me, you were telling me your name," said Katherine.

"Yes, I was," said the bat, "before you interrupted."

"I," said Katherine but the bat chimed in immediately with, "Ivanhoe."

"Oh," said Katherine, "so your name's Ivanhoe. How romantic."

"Yes, that's what my mother thought when she gave it to me. But my grandmother, fearing I'd develop illusions of grandeur and take myself too seriously, changed it to Ivanhoho. And in our culture, what the Old Bat says, goes."

"Well, ok-KAY, Ivanhoho," said Katherine, raising her eyebrows, "may I ask you a question? Everyone seems to think you know everything."

"I don't, but you may ask anyway. Even though it's the dead of day, and I should be sleeping."

"Well then, where's Mary and why can't we talk to her from outside the house?" asked Katherine bluntly.

"Hrrmmumpht," Ivanhoho cleared his throat, which to us would sound like a chirp, but which to a three-inch Katherine sounded like a choking Saint Bernard. "Mary is wherever Mary wants to be, except outside the confines of this house. For she's trapped and ensnared by these magical walls of her own making. You can't speak to her from outside because when you shrink, your voice sound frequency shifts out of the human audible range. Therefore tiny humans can *see* big humans and vice versa, but they can't *hear* each other."

"Oh," replied Katherine, the explanation being neither well understood nor completely satisfactory. Yet who should know more about sound than a bat? "About this shrinking," continued Katherine, "the mice tell me you're too old to shrink into this house when you get you're front teeth, and the cockroaches say it's when you get hair on your legs. What's the truth? And can you really get trapped in here?"

"Why do you insist on asking two or three questions at the same time?" replied the bat. "Stirs my brain too much. Still, all the answers are wrapped up in the same thing, The Harmony Code."

Here the bat stopped talking and Katherine cocked her head at him again. "So, tell me the rest," she begged, "what's this Harmony Code?"

"Ah The Harmony Code," began the bat reflectively, "it's a riddle and an explanation. It's all you need to know, and more than you can understand. It's your guide in life and your judge in death. It's your comfort in trials and a thorn in your side when you're comfortable. It's confoundingly simple and frustratingly complex. It's mysteriously revealing, captivatingly liberating, liberally conservative, obscurely obvious. It's..."

"Oh please Ivanhoho," interrupted the small girl, "your words are too big for me to understand."

The bat shrugged its angular shoulders and became silent once again. This time Katherine waited patiently with her hands folded sweetly on her lap. She rocked a little in the chair and the floor creaked monotonously. A cloud drifted slowly by outside the window.

Finally the bat began again, "You can't use small words to explain big concepts, but you can certainly use picture-talk. In fact, this house you're standing in is nothing but picture talk. Let me try to explain. You're able to be in here not because you don't have teeth or hair, but because you're so childlike."

"I'm trying to be more grown-up," said Katherine, thrusting out her chin a bit.

"Oh no, don't misunderstand," replied the bat, his folded wings quivering agitatedly. "Being childlike is a wonderful thing. You needn't rush away from it; it'll abandon you in its own good time and all too soon for you, I'm afraid. When it does you'll be left with only its vestigial ghost, childishness. And I do warn you not to get trapped in here like Mary because if it."

"Just exactly how *did* she get trapped?" asked Katherine.

"She followed her foolish ways in here, persisted in them and suddenly when she became accountable she found herself still trapped in them. Now it's humanly impossible for her to get out."

"But can't I help her get out?" asked Katherine.

The Code states that only a Kin Liberator can do that, and she's all alone in this world," said the bat. "I'm sorry if the truth hurts your feelings or violates your sense of fairness."

Katherine frowned, sighed and got up to leave. "By the way, Mister Bat," she said, "my brother William tried to get in here, but he couldn't. How come?

"Your William has entered the age of accountability and as such cannot enter here unless he fully renounces and surrenders his own internal illusions of grandeur and private pretensions to deity."

"What are you talking about?" barked Katherine.

"It's dispelling the myth of your own supreme authority. That you're your own God. Only El can be God. That's very hard for an adult to appropriate but it comes very naturally for children, in their innocence and partially unsoiled state."

"Are you saying that William can come in here if I can get him to say that he's not God?"

"If you can get him to *believe* it, he can."

Katherine gazed at the bat with its rich brown fur and funny ears. She decided she was being rude keeping it up so late in the day, so she rose from the rocking chair and headed for the door.

"Don't you want to use the window?"

"Won't I grow big as soon as I get outside on the roof and maybe crush this house?"

"Why yes, I suppose you would. Are you game to face the spiders again?"

"Not really."

"Beware of them. They feel sorry for themselves and like to make you feel sorry for them as well. They always want you to stay longer, but if you do they only talk more about their problems. They also love to prattle on about the framed pictures they live on. Take care or they'll suck you dry emotionally."

"I'd rather use a candle on them."

"Oh you needn't go that far when a small dose of flattery will do. Remember that one word is worth a thousand pictures."

So with this, Katherine said goodbye to the bat and burst resolutely back into the room full of spiders.

~14~
Silk Sewing

When Katherine opened her eyes in the tiny room nothing happened. A bolt of panic ran down her throat. "I'm blind!" she thought. But then as soon as her eyes adjusted to the gloom she was able to make out shapes, then details and then bulbous spider bodies everywhere. An involuntary shudder shook her shoulders.

But Shcandelaria immediately spied her and sung out in her sweetest, honey-like voice, "Hail girly again. Oh's, don'st be so scaredy. Nicest to see you so soon. Sorry to be so sobbing last time. Sometimes I loose myself in sorrow. Have you seen my picture here which I decorated myself in silk?"

"Oh Shcandelaria," said Katherine, grateful for the kind words, "it's simply stunning, striking – in one word, extravagant."

"Thanks sincerely," replied the baby spider. "Hey Moms did you hear what she said about my silk sewing? I must be getting better at it."

"Yes you are, my dear," replied Shirlaa, her mom.

"Do you all make these wonderful silk designs?" asked Katherine.

"It's what spiders do!" replied Shirlaa, "and it's almost time for our daily lesson. Why don't you stay and watch."

"Oh yes, yes, girly, please stay," squealed Shcandelaria, "Mom, can she work on a frame of her own like Smary? Please, please, please."

"That's is up to your greatest-great-grandmother," replied Shirlaa.

"Oh Snana, please, please?" begged the baby spider, turning to a dull, wrinkly black shape close by, with only seven legs.

"Suppose so," said the old matriarch, "since I'm already schooling Smary."

"Smary?" asked Katherine with a start, "is that Mary? Is she coming here?"

"Smary is Smary and I hear her footsteps now!" bubbled Shcandelaria, jumping up and down on all of her spindly legs.

Katherine glanced at the door through which she had entered but all the spiders began staring at her with their beady eyes. Soon she felt a thump on the floor under her feet and jumped quickly aside being extra careful not to brush against any of the spiders on the wall.

"About'st time you stepped aside to let Smary up!" said Shcandelaria.

And sure enough, a trap door opened and a girl with long brown hair and big round eyes popped her head out. She appeared a few years older than Katherine, having all her teeth and body hair too, she supposed, although she couldn't see her legs.

Suddenly all the spiders joined in sappy choruses of Hail Smarys and glads to see you but Mary was too busy staring at Katherine to return their greetings.

"*What* is *this*?" demanded Mary, addressing the spiders and not Katherine.

"It's is only Girly," said Shcandelaria, "nice girly who wants only to silk sew with us, please, please Smary."

"Well she's not *necessary*! There's no *room* in here for her. Snana, tell her to go."

The old spider, not wanting to get involved in human disputes, slunk slowly behind her picture frame, as did all her daughters, granddaughters and great-granddaughters, etc.

This left Mary to deal with Katherine herself. Katherine refused to help her out of the secret passageway and retreated to the opposite corner of the room. Mary climbed in athletically, sat down in her corner and motioned Katherine to do the same in her area. The room was so small that their knees almost touched in the middle.

"Well, since you're here, you might as well tell me your name," began Mary.

"Katherine," said Katherine in a pouty voice.

"Scasrins," echoed Shcandelaria from behind her picture frame.

"Well Scasrins," said Mary mockingly, "usually we make an effort before coming here to put on nicer clothes, comb our hair, and apply a bit of makeup. But since you're obviously not leaving, are you ready for a sewing lesson?"

Katherine set her brow and stuck out her chin a bit, but to no effect. The two girls just stared at each other until finally Mary cracked a simile and giggled a bit. "Okay, 'girly,' I'll have to admit you're easier to look at than present company – spelled, s-p-i-d-e-r-s. But just wait till you see what they've taught me."

With this, Snana gave a signal and all the spiders began spinning silk strands which dangled longer and longer from each picture frame. Mary retrieved two empty picture frames from lower off the wall and handed one to Katherine.

"First we make the basic tulle. Then we lace-stitch our design. Remember the tulle is made of concentric circles on radiating strands. That's right Smary."

Mary was daintily plucking strands of silk from the spiders and gingerly placing them across her frame. Each strand intersected in the center of the picture. Then she expertly crafted her circles, a small one in the center and then larger and larger ones until she reached the wooden frame.

Katherine, on the other hand, was still afraid to touch the spider silk, and when she did, it balled up into a sticky mass on her fingertips. "I can't do this," she said, "it's icky."

"If we didn't bite our nails, we'd be able to better handle the silk," said Mary acidly.

Katherine banged the frame angrily on her knees and started again. Finally she got three strands awkwardly in place and inspected them with pride. The threads were almost invisible in the dim light.

Mary, working swiftly and accurately, finished her tulle, which looked exactly like many other spider webs. But then she began laying stitches on this base with either a simple loop or an extra twist. She then added rows built upon the first by grouping stitches in sets of two or three above the previous rows. All the while she kept staring at Katherine and then glancing back down at her work.

This unsettled Katherine because her own work was so crude and untidy. She had so much loose silk hanging everywhere in clumps, that the spiders were getting hesitant to give her more. Even Shcandelaria was beginning to chuckle at her.

At last Mary finished her piece and showed it to Snana.

"Mary, you've outdone yourself this time. I've never seen better."

"May I give it to her?" asked Mary.

"You know we normally just stick them to the walls and reuse the frames. Can you bring us another frame?"

"I think so."

"Alright then. Can you two girls stay a while and chat?"

"Well no, sorry," replied Mary, "the mice are expecting me for a charm school lesson and punctuality is a big part of my grade." Mary glanced at Katherine. "You didn't come up those awful, dusty stairs did you? Come, would you like to use my secret passageway? You can keep a secret, can't you?"

"Oh sure, bye bye Snana, Shirlaa, and you too Shcandelaria," said Katherine.

"Seeings you's later," said Mary.

"Until sooners or slaters," said all the spiders in unison and the two girls disappeared down the hole in the floor. Just before they closed the trap door, however, Mary took a small jar from her purse and released a fair number of frantic and frenzied flies into the air.

~15~
The Etiquette Lesson

The two girls emerged from a secret panel in Mary's bedroom and inspected each other in adequate light for the first time. Mary was a fair bit taller, and her hair was much lighter than it had appeared upstairs. Also Katherine noted that her eyes were a striking green. She had smooth skin, not as pasty white as Katherine's and a soft, pleasing smile. All in all she looked like a refined young lady while Katherine still pictured herself as a little kid. She wished she could have her new front teeth at least.

Mary was still carrying the picture she'd made, so Katherine asked to see it.

"Sure you can see it," said Mary, "it's yours. A gift from me to you."

"Oh my," said Katherine, and then, "OH MY!" she added as she saw what it was.

The room brought out the richness and sophistication of the piece and it shimmered and iridesced in the light. Part of it was transparent, part had a milky translucence, and part was a reflective satin which picked up the color of the small girl's cheeks and eyes. The detail was so fine that your eyes could get lost in its intricacy.

But the most striking thing about the work was that it was a portrait of herself, Katherine, in faithful but pleasing rendition, and with full appreciation her countenance. It masterfully captured and even enhanced her likeness and essence.

But so fragile. The spiders just make them and then paste them up on their walls on top of the previous ones. They don't appreciate their genius or preserve their industry. It all becomes wall plaster.

"Are you ready for your bubble bath?" asked Mary, breaking into Katherine's reverie.

"Bubble bath?"

You can't take your etiquette lesson as dirty as you appear to be. I take six bubble baths daily. You owe it to yourself. You owe it to me. Don't forget to wash behind your ears. Do you need me to help you?"

Katherine frowned and fitfully endured her bubble bath, even eventually washing her hair and behind her ears. The bath ended up being so luxurious that she lingered until the water became cold and every bubble had disappeared. While she was in the tub Mary washed, dried, and ironed her clothes.

Finally suitably perfumed and otherwise presentable the pair approached the door to the drawing room where Luucy awaited at the precisely appointed hour.

"Young ladies," she began, "I see you have become acquainted. That is so commendable. Remember that common courtesy is really so much more imperative than the deep quagmires of friendship – façade more important than fiber – masks more essential than morals. So here, let's review our ten principles of charm.

The Ten Principles of Charm [4]

1. Charm is the ability to make someone think that both of you are quite wonderful.

2. Beauty is an emotional reaction – the effect we have on other people. It is 70% personality, 20% posture, and 10% appearance. Its number one element is facial expression in humans and smell in everyone else..

3. Smiling improves circulation which improves complexion. Frowning cuts off blood flow to the face and causes pimples.

4. Carry breath fresheners with you and use them often. Give them to your friends as well.

5. Be cordial. Speak and act as if everything you do is a genuine pleasure, even if it isn't.

6. Be prodigious with praise, cautious with criticism, and stingy with scorn.

7. Leg position when sitting: knees tight together, ankles crossed and tucked to the side the front leg is on."

Here the mouse stopped and remarked, "I've always had trouble with that one myself, but these rules are only loose guidelines for rodents and not applicable at all for snakes. Anyway…

8. Care for your skin," she continued, "you only get one. Your appearance is the greatest evidence of what you think of yourself.

9. Remember, some prints look better on your wall than on your particular figure type!

10. Negative self image produces an inability to trust El."

Just about this time Katherine did something very rude indeed. She glanced out the window. She did this because two figures outside caught the corner of her eye. They were heading over to the castle and if she craned her neck she could see them trying to enter. It didn't take long to recognize them as her brothers and she began wondering if William would get in this time. He didn't seem to be succeeding and James kept remonstrating at him with arm gestures and shaking his head.

"Katherine, would you like to share with us what is so fascinating outside and more important than our lesson?" demanded Luucy.

Mary looked over at the window as well. "Why, isn't that taller boy the peeping Tom who gawked at me in my bathrobe this morning?" she said.

"Hey," protested Katherine, "that's my brother William you're talking about. And besides he doesn't gawk at girls. He's not interested in them at all."

"Oh, go on," scoffed Mary, "boys that big are always interested in girls."

"Not him, he still plays with frogs," said Katherine.

"Uh, excuse me," Luucy cut in again, "perhaps we should put away our lesson until tomorrow. If that is fine with you two girls and doesn't conflict with your boy-gawking activities. Stop considering men anyway. Take it from me, men are all the same, overrated and unchanging. Besides, if men became what we wanted, we wouldn't want them. You'll be here again soon, won't you Katherine dear?"

"Oh yes, of course. I'll be back, but first I want to show William my picture here. Hey Mary would you like me to introduce you to him?"

"Not if he has frog slime on his hands," said Mary.

"Oh, I'll clean him up for sure; come on lets go."

"Aren't you forgetting something?" said Mary, "I can't leave this building."

"Well I really must be going," injected Luucy, "dinners don't make themselves." With this she padded out the door, being careful to look back at them and try her best to smile, an effort which only succeeded in making her look silly.

Katherine looked into Mary's eyes. "Oh you poor thing, that's right, you're trapped in here. Okay, I'll try to bring William here to you."

"Oh you needn't put yourself out on my account. In fact I really wouldn't know what to do with something like a boy in here. Would he enjoy cross-stitch or flute lessons? Ha-ha. Maybe we should just forget it."

"Why Mary, I do think you're blushing," said Katherine.

"I most certainly am not," said Mary. "It's this special rouge on my cheeks. Made from butterfly-wing powder. Go ahead and invite him in. Why should I care? As long as you tell him not to gawk at me."

~16~
The Little Queen

As Katherine turned to leave the mansion and was about to barge through the massive front door, she noticed a bee trapped inside by one of the antique rippled glass panes. It was busy buzzing fruitlessly trying to get out into the light. Finally, exhausted it alighted on the door knob near Katherine's nose just as her hand was about to grab it.

"Whoa," she exclaimed, "hornet here!"

"Not hornet," said Mary, "That looks more like a honeybee."

"Yes, indeed," it said in a violin-like voice, "but actually I'm a very young queen honeybee lost on my honeymoon flight and about to die here of embarrassment."

"Oh my," said Mary, "do you want us to let you out?"

"Oh yes – I guess. No wait. I don't think so. Here I am on my honeymoon and I'm trapped in here and I've lost all my bee-man pursuers."

"So what," said Mary acidly, "we don't need men in here. Bee-men, spider-men, or even men-men."

This agitated the bee even more. "We always need men, girlfriend, but I've lost all mine and I can't start a new hive without one."

"Oh sure you can, see what a nice household we have here without men."

"It's different in a hive! We need men! At least one of them, if you know what I mean."

"She doesn't," said Katherine, changing the subject, "do you have a name, miss bee?"

"Well yes, my child, my name is HM Mae Bea."

"Well HM Mae Bea," said Mary, "I'm interested to know what's so great about men, and why you think we need them."

"Okay, okay, *we* call them drones and they're chunky, cheeky little things who eat us out of hive and home and do no work at all in return. They buzz on and on about every subject imaginable and fancy themselves great warriors and song writers, but they have no clout, no sting, and no talent."

"I see. So what does your HM stand for?" asked Katherine.

"Why Her Majesty, of course. I'm surprised you didn't notice my royal bearing and breeding, but you don't need to curtsey since you aren't a bee. Would you like to know more about being a queen though? Never mind, of course you would. Some day you may become queens yourselves. Of course you will."

So her majesty stretched her wings, neatly folded them across her back and then began. "I am a queen by birthright and upbringing, forever majestic and regal. Therefore I live by these ten simple rules. You should take them to heart because they will serve you well in life.

The Queen Bee Philosophy

1. You are the most important person in your own personal hive, so act like it.

2. Always be the center of attention. Assemble lots of worker bees around you and let them hang on your every word and command.

3. Stand out in a crowd. Be bigger and better.

4. Be a picky eater. Only eat royal jelly.

5. Always act and dress to attract males.

6. Fly high and let the males pursue you. They will.

7. But make sure only the best boy overtakes you high in the air.

8. When he does catch you, don't fight him off.

9. When times get tough get rid of him, and all other males in your life. Concentrate on your babies.

10. Destroy all other queens in your life."

"My, that's quite a good philosophy," said Mary, but Katherine wasn't so sure. She quickly opened the door, letting the bee out and then herself. Instantly, of course she sprang up to full size and forgot all about the tiny bee which must have made its way back to the backyard. Katherine peered back through the window at Mary and smiled. Mary smiled back, then cocked her head and motioned for her to start over toward the two boys.

~17~
Getting Me In

"You're doing it all wrong," whined James at my attempts to enter the castle. "You're not wishing hard enough!"

"I *am* wishing!" I hissed. "I'm wishing you'd shut up long enough for me to wish properly. I wish, I wish, I *wish*. See. Still nothing happens. I'm wishing till my veins pop out."

"William," said James more quietly, "it's not just wishing, it's believing too. Remember what the rats said. Do you believe you can get in?"

"You got in, didn't you," I said, "of course I believe."

"Hey wait," said James, "I know – of course! We need to believe and *pray*."

That sounded funny to me, but we tried it nevertheless and again, nothing happened. I started to feel a little guilty about praying that God would shrink me so I could enter a toy castle with my retarded brother.

Just about this time Katherine appeared in a flash outside the door to the mansion. She strolled over to the castle where we boys were standing.

"What's wrong fellas?" she inquired mockingly.

James tried to shove her aside and turned back to me. Maybe there's not enough of us wishing and believing, he said. "Yeah, that's it. Hey kids! Yeah, you kids reading this book. You know we want William to get into the castle with us so please, please won't you wish him in with us. Yes, that's it. Wish. Wish. Okay, if you're really wishing and believing please clap your hands. That's right clap. Yeah clap. Clap Clap. I think it's working. Clap. Clap Clap. Oh, it must be working. I *believe* it's working."

"James, you're making an idiot of yourself," hooted Katherine. "Look at you, nothing's working, is it?"

"Well, so what?" cried James, "you must be jinxing it."

"I am not," said Katherine, "but I do have the real secret to getting inside."

"What's that?" I asked immediately.

"Surrender," said Katherine. "The old bat told me if you're old enough to think you're high and mighty, if you think you're so great you don't need God any more, then you're in for trouble. For instance, you can't get in or out of impossible places if you won't let God make it happen for you."

"But we prayed?"

"The bat says that prayers aren't magic words that can command doors to open for you."

"Who is this bat anyway?" I bellowed, "He's certainly full of definite ideas, isn't he? Oh well, letting God do all the work sounds much easier than wishing and believing yourself into the castle – so, ok God, *let me in*."

I thrust my hand into the castle but nothing happened.

So I tried again, only louder. "OKAY GOD, LET ME IN!"

Again, I thrust my hand into the castle, deeper this time, but still nothing happened. In fact I got it stuck and James and Katherine had to coax it out with their tiny fingers.

"I've had enough of this foolishness," I said, and I shooed the other two out of the room and down the stairs. James headed out to the backyard in a huff, but Katherine grabbed my arm with her fingernails and roughly led me into the small den. Then she shoved me down on the loveseat with her strong, wiry arms and bounced down beside me, this time banging her heels down in my lap.

"Are you missing part of your brain?" she bristled.

"What are you talking about?"

"You should've been able to get into that castle. The bat told me exactly how to get in and he knows everything."

"Well maybe he forgot a thing or two," I said. "I'm not sure I believe in your bat anyway. Sounds like you're believing too much in figments of your own imagination."

"It's not fig mints of my imagination! I can *prove* it." She proceeded to retrieve the silk-lace portrait of herself from her pocket and reverently handed it to me. Unfortunately, here in the outside world, it was only the size of a postage stamp.

"So what?" I said cruelly, fingering it. "This looks like a toy. Why is it sticky?"

"Hey, don't put your thumb through it, it's a picture of me made out of spider webs."

He shot me an incredulous look. "Doesn't look like that to me. I don't believe it. That's impossible."

"Well it's true anyway. You don't have to believe it, for it to be true. Say," said Katherine, grabbing it back and returning it carefully to her pocket. "Say, that could be it. I know why you can't get in the castle. James said wish and believe, but the bat said surrender. Why don't you try surrendering *and* believing."

"Oh, you mean surrendering in your *heart* and not just your head?" I asked.

"Bingo," she clapped, springing off the loveseat and pulling my arm, "Come on, lets try it."

"No," I said, getting up slowly and pushing her back down on the seat. "Katherine, this is something I need to do all by myself. Will you stay here nicely and listen to the radio or something? I'll be back shortly."

She stuck out her lower lip but nodded her head consentingly in my direction. "You'll tell me all about it?" she purred.

"You'll be the first to know."

Somehow I knew in my heart I would get in this time. My secret aim was to bring something *out* of the castle, like a sword or a chest of gold. No telling *what* they had stashed in there. I leaned down over the drawbridge, but in doing so caught a glimpse of the mansion in the corner of my eye. And sure enough, there in a window was that spy girl gawking at my backside. Completely disconcerted, and not wanting to appear foolish in front of her, I went over to her window and stared straight in. Surprisingly she didn't retreat but just beamed right back into my eyes.

That was awkward because I was banking on the fact that she would be true to form and retreat into the dark recesses of some secret passageway. Now instead, she was holding my gaze and I was the one who felt like retreating. So I did what any self-respecting gentleman my age would do. I smiled stupidly, quickly ducked out of the way, and snuck over to the front door but was afraid to knock. I tried to look through the rippled glass but my head was too big to get down that low. Suddenly the door opened from inside and I tumbled in, head-over-backside into an inglorious heap on the throw rug. Amazingly and effortlessly I was inside! She helped me up, to my extreme embarrassment. We were exactly the same size and this must have disconcerted her, for once again she put her hand to her mouth, turned and disappeared in a series of fading footsteps down a hall. I tried to follow but soon became lost in a labyrinth of turning corridors and passageways. Presently, however, I came upon a secret panel in a wall. It had been hastily left partway open so I went in and followed its narrow stairs up and up. At the very top there were three doors. I eyed each one in speculation, wondering what lay behind each. Finally, I opened the first one carefully and peered into a room containing only a spinning wheel, a three-legged stool, and a huge pile of fine lambs wool. But no sign of Mary. Behind the second door was a wonderful old harpsichord with page after page of yellowing sheet music. Most had pencil markings on them denoting fingering or timing. But still no sign of Mary, although her name appeared atop some of the pages. For sure she'd be behind the third door so I barged in forcefully half hoping to throw her off balance.

But I was in for a rude surprise.

~18~
I Confront the Bat

Unfortunately, when I burst into the room, what I threw off balance was not a fleeing maiden, but a bat, which fluttered about in a panic past my hair yelling, "chee, chee, chee." I later learned this means 'crap' in bat, and is a very rude thing to say. You would never say it, would you? But the bat certainly did. "Chee, chee, chee," it continued screaming. "Chee, chee, chee. – Chee, chee, chee!"

"Alright already," I fumed to myself.

When it finally settled down it eyed me suspiciously.

"Who might you be?" it said.

I was so surprised to hear a bat talk that I didn't respond.

"Who – might – you – be?" it repeated, this time as if to an idiot or imbecile.

"I am a boy," I said stupidly.

"Oh, a boy! Why, I thought you were an elephant. Of course you're a boy. By 'who' I was asking after your name."

"William," I said, "what's yours?"

"Resolute Guardian," said the bat pensively.

"Is that you're name?" I asked.

"No, it's yours. Never mind mine, it's embarrassing. You can call me Ivan for short. What brings you up here to my loft?"

"I was looking for Mary."

"Ah, everyone's favorite person, Mary. You're not here to carry her off as a wife or concubine are you?"

I tried to stifle a gasp but only succeeded in spraying the bat.

"I'll take that as a no," he said. "And my daily bath. Alright then. What are you here for?"

"Well actually Mister Bat, I was wondering if you could explain to me why Mary is trapped in this house."

"Well it's a long story, will you settle for the short version?"

"Any version will do."

"Okay Mister Boy here goes.

"Mary first came in here much the same age as the new girl, Katherine, but…"

"She's my sister," I interrupted.

"Oh, how charming, do you want to hear the story or do you want to give me your family tree?"

"Sorry, please continue."

"Well as I was *saying*, Mary came in here at a very young age, emotionally at least, and became fascinated with all the wonderful things to learn and do in here.

98

Eventually she became masterful in all the fine and practical arts of accomplished young ladies. But somewhere along the way she became quite addicted to perfection and found herself lost to the outside real-world. She is now beginning to have trouble with the imperfections of others. Mind you, she is a wonderful person, she's just trapped in her own personal follies and foibles. The Harmony Code, which governs us all, whether we like it or not, dictates that when a young person reaches a critical age they become accountable for over-indulging in such follies and they become addicted to, or captivated by them. Entrapped."

"Is there no escape?" I asked.

"None. Oh, but I must tell the whole truth. There is one way out but it involves a Kin Liberator, of which she has none."

"Why not?" I asked.

"Because she has no kin, like I plainly said."

"How does it work then? If I may ask."

"Well, if a Kin Liberator who is not similarly trapped can break into their confidence, their shell of folly, and then persuade them to break out, then the cycle is broken. Only the Kin Liberator then becomes trapped, taking on the punishment due the original offending person."

"Oh my, does Mary know all this?" I asked.

"She knows very little about the deeper meanings of The Harmony Code. She has no desire to leave this place. And part of me doesn't blame her at all. She is very beautiful and innocent, as you can plainly see. The outside world is exceptionally cruel to such as these."

"But at least the outside world is real," I countered.

"Yes, I suppose you are correct there. But being correct to the letter is not superior to being right in principle, and being right is not better than being loving."

"Have you heard of 'tough love?'" I asked.

"Tough love is the name by which some people impose their own wills on the unwilling," said the bat.

"Well thank you for your time, Ivan," I said, wrinkling my brow and wondering. "Before I go could you tell me where Mary might be hiding?"

"Oh, I don't think she's hiding from you at all. I think you'll find her always just one step ahead of you."

"Then how can I catch her?"

"You don't have to. Don't try."

~19~
The Fainting Sofa

After leaving the bat's lair, I trundled down the stairs and sure enough, soon caught a glimpse of a door closing down a dark hall. I followed into a room and through a secret panel left ajar. There was the smell of sweet perfume in the still air. Soon I spied a skirt whisking around a distant corner and I set after it. But of course it had eluded me again.

After about an hour of this cat and mouse game I remembered what Ivan had said about chasing her. So the next time I was led through a room with a place to sit down, I did just that. It happened to be a lovely open room dominated by an ornately carved fainting sofa. It was six feet long with a rich mahogany finish and button tufting all across its cream-colored, gracefully curved back.

Not long after I'd sat down, a bookcase in the wall pivoted on its center and a slim body slipped gracefully through. Mary had changed into a modest yellow sun dress. Her hair, brushed back into a ponytail, swung saucily as she approached and alighted daintily on the far edge of the fainting couch.

"So here's where you're hiding," she said, avoiding my gaze.

"I'm not hiding. I was just taking a break on this loveseat here."

"It's not a loveseat," she said blushing. "It's a fainting sofa. A fainting sofa is always essential for graceful reclining in a formal setting."

"Are you going to faint?" I asked.

"Of course not, are you?"

"Men don't faint."

"I don't suppose they do. They just get knocked out by things. Why are you here? Are you going to try to carry me off somewhere?"

"Of course not! Do I look like some kind of monster?"

"My tutors say that it's the beasts which turn out to be princes and the handsome princes which turn out to be beasts. I think I'd like to know what your intensions are."

"I'm not here to hurt you."

"You couldn't anyway. I have many guardians within these walls and I have a green belt in Karate under this yellow dress."

"I'm sure you do. But Ivan tells me you're sweet and loving."

"Ivan?" she said, laughing, "you mean Ivanhoho?"

Now it was my turn to laugh. "That's an odd name."

"It's a long story, do you want the short version?"

"We both smiled at the same time."

"What I'd really like to know is if you really like it in here. Don't you get lonely?" I said.

"I have many quality friends."

"Like the bat?"

"Yes, like him, and others."

"But do you know any people?"

"They *are* people."

"I mean *human* people."

"Well, there's Katherine. I think she might like to live in here with me."

"I wouldn't count on it, she's my sister," I said.

"Oh, so that makes you the boss of her?"

"It means I take care of her and letting her get trapped in here is not my idea of taking care of her. Haven't you ever wondered what's outside these walls?"

"I was out there before," she remarked, "but I don't remember much and do wonder if things have changed."

"People have grown up, for one thing."

"I'm grown up. Would you like me to make you something even as we sit here?"

"What can you make without any instruments or supplies?" I asked.

"Well I can make this:" she said.

"There once was a Willy from the moors,
Who chased a poor Mary through the floors;
In circles they went,
Until he was spent,
And ended up crawling on all fours."

I didn't know what to think of this. All I ended up saying was, "Don't call me Willy."

"Why not. It's short for William, isn't it?

"How do you know my name anyway?"

"Katherine told me. She told me everything about you. I know when you stopped sucking your thumb."

"Maybe I still do, why should you care?"

"I don't."

"I think you do, to remember everything about me like that."

She stood up and walked purposefully to the window. "Is the garden out there as pretty as it used to be?" she demanded.

"Prettier," I guessed in reply, not knowing what it had looked like before, "there's a goldfish pond and birds nesting in the ivy."

"Oh," she said, "I haven't seen a bird in... Do they still come in so many colors?"

"All colors of the rainbow and they sing as sweetly as they look."

"How would you know? All you do is dive for slimy frogs."

"Frogs are the birds of the lily pond and sliminess is meaningless under water. Their songs fill the night air."

She turned and looked at me with a surprised look. "Could you take me for just a short walk in this garden and then bring me right back here?"

I almost fainted on the fainting sofa.

"I'm not going to ask twice," she said.

"Well, sure I'd be honored to try," I replied.

"Try?" she said, "Are you unsure of your capabilities as a gentleman to take a lady for a walk in the garden?"

"Well, I mean, you..." my voice trailed off.

She was already strolling to the front door and stood beside it. "Are you going to make me open it myself?" she asked.

Suddenly all the warnings about The Harmony Code and entrapment came back to me. Was I playing with fire here? Was this what I really wanted to do? I wasn't certain what was going to happen, but it would probably be unpleasant. Still, the thought of Mary strolling among the butterflies in the garden chased all the fears out of my mind.

I walked in a daze over to where she was standing until I could smell the very fragrance of her. She tilted her head at me ever so slightly. I glanced into those big green eyes, grabbed the door handle and said in the bravest tone I could muster, "After you, Mary."

~20~
Mary Gets Free

Mary walked boldly out of the dollhouse and immediately burst into her full size. It almost threw her off balance but she regained her feet and then her composure. She inspected herself and felt for her ponytail. It was still there, thank goodness – for what good is a girl without her hair? She thought of letting it down, for she might be meeting new people out here and first impressions are everything. So she did let it down and shook her head so it swirled gracefully about her shoulders. Now she wished she'd wore something more formal than this old yellow sun dress. Oh well, a sun dress would be appropriate for a short stroll in the garden. Where was William anyway? A lady should always have an escort in the garden.

She turned back to peer into the door but couldn't see anything. That's because I'd bounced nose-first off the space filling the open door as if it had been a wall of bullet-proof glass. I tried to leave again but this time hurt my elbow. After several attempts in quick succession and a brief panic attack, I went over to the window and regarded Mary's huge legs outside. All I could see were her calves, which looked like two tree trunks. Please don't ever tell her that I compared her legs to tree trunks, okay? Anyway, I thrust open the window to touch them but couldn't reach out. I yelled at her but to no avail. It was horrible and embarrassing. Finally she noticed me popping up and down like a tiny jack-in-the-box. She bent over and peered in.

Her face looked alarmed and then sad. She poked her graceful long fingers in the window at me but they didn't shrink. This made her look alarmed again and she tried the same thing with the door. No dice, she didn't shrink.

When she eventually came back to the window she looked perplexed and then angry. I got the distinct impression she was mad at *me* for making her go out. Does shaking a fist at someone mean that they're mad? Well, I didn't shove her out or anything, did I? I kept motioning her to go downstairs and get someone to help but she just stood there with her hands on her hips. As if I could magically snap my fingers and fix everything. In fact, this whole thing was getting out of hand. I didn't really relish being trapped in this dollhouse even one more minute. Tomorrow was a school day and I had a report due.

Finally she glared into my eyes, set her brow and turned toward the door leading out of the room. On her way over to it she noticed the bed and wondered if this was all just a bad dream. Maybe if she laid down there and went to sleep she would wake up. Perhaps in another dimension she was actually asleep on that bed. Perhaps we are all living in an allusion. What if we are just a figment of God's imagination? A broken teacup crunching under her feet brought her back to reality. She tried the pretty glass doorknob. It turned easily and she slipped through silently. At the bottom of the stairs was a landing and a lot of bedrooms. Not wanting to disturb anyone in bed, or worse, in a bubble bath, she descended the second staircase and turning, spied the hallway leading to the backyard door.

She followed the calming, yellow sunlight out into a magnificent symphony of green leaves and vivid, fragrant flowers. They were so stimulating she forgot to breathe in the warm, clean air. "Oh" she gasped as she ambled along the path. "Oh my." She spun slowly as she walked, dazzled at the splendor and noticing that the stirring clouds were shaped like animals. Eventually her foot slid off the path. "Oh my!" she repeated and hopped back.

"Who are you? Are you drunk?" came a voice from behind, rudely breaking her reverie.

"I'm the goddess princess of this garden," she said when she realized the voice was coming from a small boy only two-thirds her size and spattered with mud.

"Are you really a princess?" he said, "princess of what?"

"I'm a fairy princess of a faraway castle called Levancrieff but now I'm lost in this forest and can't find my way home."

"Levancrieff! I know where that is. Do you know the noble knight Sherwoode?"

This shocked Mary. "Well, actually I'm not of the castle, but of the house next door," she said, "have you been there too?"

"No, but I can take you there, I know where it is."

"Could you get in?"

"Oh sure. I can get in the castle, can't I."

"Well, lets go then," said Mary.

James led her back inside and as they were heading toward the stairs Mary spied Katherine through an open door.

"Never mind her," James whined, "she's just the servant girl..."

"But I already *know* her," snapped Mary, "that's Katherine, your sister. Hey Katherine, come on. I'm trapped outside Mousumerset Manor."

"How did *that* happen?" asked Katherine as they were climbing the stairs with a petulant James in tow.

"Well, Willy made a mistake and let me out and now he's trapped inside."

"Who's Willy?" piped James from behind.

"Not my *brother*?" demand Katherine.

"One and the same," said Mary, "that's my pet name for him."

Katherine stopped in mid-step. "What have you done to him?" she rasped.

"*Nothing*! He was going to take me for a walk in the garden but now he can't get out and *I can't get back in*!"

"I know how to get you in," said the voice from behind, but neither of the girls paid the slightest attention to it.

But sure enough, after an hour of trying there was nothing Katherine could do to get William out or Mary back in. She even tried getting them to "surrender" themselves, but somehow it didn't work this time.

So again James piped up, "I *said* – I know how to do it."

This time the girls turned to face him. "Might as well let him try," said Mary to Katherine.

"He's never been right before," said Katherine to Mary.

"Well *you're* not getting it done!" said Mary to Katherine.

"Okay James, show us then," they both barked at him.

"Kath, you must come with me," said James with a new air of authority. "Mary, you stay right here and keep William company. Don't let him smash anything until I get back. And don't wander back down into the garden. I think you're allergic to it."

So James and his sister left Mary alone, to primp her hair and peer in at William from time to time. The siblings headed resolutely toward the castle and had no trouble entering it with a snap. Getting *out* would prove to be much more difficult.

~21~
Big Trouble in the Castle

"Careful on these steps, someone could get killed, and it might be me," warned James.

"If this is a wild goose chase, I'm going to kill you myself," said Katherine, addressing the back of his legs on the way up the circular staircase. "Where *are* we going anyway?"

"To get Woodiekins, he'll know what to do."

"You mean *you* don't!"

"I said I could get her in, I didn't say I already knew how I would do it."

Katherine tried to kick him but almost lost her balance on the steps.

"Besides," continued James, "what's the big deal about getting her back in there anyway? She could come live with us."

"It's not getting her *in* I'm worried about, it's getting William *out*!"

"Oh, I suppose so. Will we all get out of school tomorrow if he's still stuck in there?" asked James.

Before Katherine had time to answer they came out into the great hall which seemed by its very nature to command silence. There was the huge fireplace. There was the massive oak table and the eight chairs. And there lying in the corner was the greatsword Logokrataioo.

"Hey," thought James to himself, "I don't need Woodiekins after all. All I need is that greatsword. It has magic in it."

Unfortunately, sitting at the table were two enormous rat-guards with greatswords of their own strapped to their sides. In addition they had a few odd daggers stuck in their belts and one even had a spare sword hanging down. Would they be friendly? The swords said no and their tone of voice confirmed it.

"And just where do you two tot-bugs think you're going?" said one of them. I forget which, but it doesn't really matter. Either could just as easily have said it. Maybe they both did.

"We're not tot-bugs," protested James, but the rats only laughed.

"Then you're tot-worms," they said.

"We've come to see Sherwoode, if you please," James announced.

"Well we don't please," replied the rats, "what business could you possibly have with the prince?"

"The prince?" James replied in astonishment, "go summon him at once or he'll have your head!"

"He doesn't like to be awakened," said a rat.

"I know, but he'll be even more displeased if you don't announce to him that we're here."

"Are you royal turtles or something?"

"Yes," interjected Katherine, "we're royal turtles with mutant mean streaks and snappy personalities. So you better get going pronto."

The rats glanced at each other and one decided to go wake the prince.

Meanwhile James and Katherine sauntered casually over to the corner where Logokrataioo lay. They regarded it from the corners of their eyes and then peered at each other. "We don't have much time," James whispered.

"I can hold up my end," said Katherine, "you take the point."

So when the remaining rat guard had momentarily put his head down on the table the two children silently picked up the sword and began to slowly, carefully inch their way across the floor with it.

James could hold up the point quite well but Katherine struggled a bit with the giant hilt. It was uncomfortable on her shoulder. Nevertheless, they got it all the way across the floor without disturbing the napping rat. So James started backwards down the stairwell and Katherine followed, pulling on the sword with all her might to prevent it from crushing her brother. The sword was almost too long to negotiate the curve of the stairwell. As it was, it scraped the wall from time to time.

"James, don't let it touch the walls," fussed Katherine in an insistent whisper.

"Stop letting it fall, hold it up," replied James even more insistently.

"I *am* holding it up; you're not guiding it properly."

"Am so, you think you could do better at this end?"

"Wait, put it down. I'm taller, let me have the point."

As soon as they laid the sword down, however, it started to slide down the steps. They tried to step on it but only succeeded in losing their balance. So the sword proceeded to clatter all the way down to the next level, with the two scrambling and tumbling after it.

"Ouch and drat!" said James, not in a whisper this time and rubbing his head tentatively, "now look what you've done. The whole castle must be awake now."

"Stop complaining and pick it up," said Katherine. "Let's run for the drawbridge, I can hear that guard coming down the steps after us."

"Katherine, your arm is bleeding," said James.

"You don't say! I must have cut it on the sword on my way down. Never mind, it doesn't hurt."

Nevertheless, James pulled a white handkerchief from his pocket and tied it snuggly around the wound.

Then they quickly picked up the sword and started running across the floor towards the massive door that led to the drawbridge. James was leading with the point of the sword firmly under his arm. Katherine was trying to run desperately holding the hilt in one hand and extending her other arm out for balance. She had to flail it about in the air to keep herself from sprawling all over the floor.

Suddenly and unexpectedly the door swung open and a wide-eyed, fat rat-guard appeared, in a white cape, dagger in hand. Katherine tried to stop herself but James instinctively drove the point of the sword into the rat's ample belly.

"Now look what you've done," said Katherine. I think the poor rat is dead."

"POOR RAT?" bellowed James, "Look he's armed with a short sword. He was going to kill us."

"That's not a short sword, you twit," screamed Katherine. "That's a kitchen knife! Look he's wearing an apron. He's a cook!"

"Well that's not my fault," said James, "come on, we've got to get out of here."

Katherine glared at him and knelt down by the struggling rat. "Look, he's not dead," she cried. She ripped off his white apron, wadded it up and held it firmly against his belly to stop the bleeding. "You'll be okay," she said, but the rat fainted.

"Come *on* Katherine!" yelled James tugging at the sword.

"I'm not going to let this rat die," said Katherine. "You go ahead. You can drag the sword behind you if you want."

"Katherine, they'll kill you."

"Get out of here James," screamed his sister as the rat-guards came bursting down the steps.

Somehow James found new strength and managed to pull Logokrataioo all the way through the guard house, under the portcullis and over the drawbridge, clear of the castle.

Meanwhile no less than five vicious-looking rat-guards now stood poised, daggers in hand over Katherine and the wounded rat.

~22~
Using the Sword

"Kill the murdering tot-bug," said the largest and ugliest of the rat-guards, pricking the point of his dagger through the fine hair at the back of Katherine's neck.

"Not so fast, Ratsputum," said another, "she's wearing the white and red arm-band of a combat-nurse."

"But she's on the *other side*," chimed in Ratatouille.

"Well that's true. Can we kill an enemy nurse?"

"Maybe we should ask," said Ratatat.

"We could kill her and say it was a mistake," said Rattan.

"Yes, lets kill her and say we didn't know she was a nurse until it was too late," said Ratsputum.

"Wait, the red spot on her armband is getting bigger," said Ratatat.

"I don't think it's an armband at all, I think it's a bandage," said Ratatouille.

"Then she's not a nurse at all!" said Rattan, drawing his second dagger.

"Then lets kill her!" said Ratsputum.

"I think *not*!" came a booming voice of authority from across the room. Put away your weapons. All of them. This is not an enemy."

"Yes, prince Sherwoode," said the rats obediently, "but she looks like an enemy leach or something, doesn't she?"

"I'm not a leach, I'm trying to *stop* the flow of blood," said Katherine, addressing the prince. "It was an accident. We didn't mean to do it."

"Look, she has no front teeth!" said Ratsputum. "Leaches have round suckers instead of teeth."

Sherwoode ignored him and addressed Katherine, "So girl, you admit you stabbed him?"

"Yes, we were trying to borrow your sword Logokrataioo, but your guards got all bent out of shape over it."

"What do humans call borrowing without asking? We call it stealing."

"But we had no time to ask. My brother William is trapped in Mousumerset Manor and we need to get him out."

"And the sword would help you how?"

"It smashes things, I'm told."

"For sure it does that, but it still belongs here in Levancrieff. If I let you go, do you promise to bring it back?"

"Yes, oh yes, I promise," pleaded Katherine.

"Then you may go, but bring Logokrataioo back with you."

"I give you my word," pledged Katherine.

As she was getting up to leave she noticed the cook-rat was not bleeding anymore. In fact the wound seemed to be quite shallow and he had regained consciousness. "Would you like a nice piece of rye bread before you leave?" he asked Katherine.

But she was already scurrying out the door. If she'd had a tail it would have been between her legs.

Meanwhile as James exited the castle he was disappointed that the greatsword didn't grow as much as he did. In fact it didn't grow at all. As such, it would be useless as a tool to smash a way to get Mary back into the mansion.

"You took all that time to get a *toothpick*?" said Mary, "what good will *that* do?"

"This toothpick," replied James, "I mean this *sword* is magic. Just watch this! *Hey sword, smash open a door for Mary.*"

After a pause in which absolutely nothing happened, Mary threw up her hands and exclaimed, "Watch what? Anyway, where's Katherine?"

"SMASH! PIERCE! STICK!" said James, louder this time.

"That thing couldn't stick an olive!" said Mary, "I *asked* – where's Katherine?"

"She's still in the castle attending to some business. She'll be along shortly. I better take this sword inside the mansion where it will be its correct size."

So James entered Mousumerset Manor, shrunk in size, and dragged the greatsword over to where I was standing.

"Here, use this," he said.

"To do what?" I asked.

"Smash your way out."

Okay, I could barely pick up the sword but succeeded in banging it against the door and windows a few times. It was like hitting a stone wall and I managed to twist my wrist painfully.

"You're crazy," I said.

"But it's a magic sword. The rats said its name means 'word power.' You should try to use it that way," said James.

I peered at him sideways, but in desperation, called out in a strong voice, "Magic sword of steel, I invoke your power to smash through this door." But the thing only bounced off the wood.

"Magic sword of strength," I tried again, "I invoke your power to smash through this window." But the thing only bounced off the glass.

"Magic sword of whatever," I tried a third time, "I invoke your power to break through this wall." But the blade only bounced off the plaster.

I was so exhausted now that I dropped the thing on my toe. "Little brother, your sword is no better than a stick." I said.

Just then Katherine barged in.

"What happened to your arm?" I asked immediately.

"Never mind, isn't the sword working?" she demanded.

James whined, "We tried everything, and it doesn't act like it's supposed to."

"We'd better go see the bat then," said Katherine.

"Bat? Not that bat again!" I exclaimed.

~23~
The Bat Speaks Again

Mary's huge eye followed us from window to window as we made our way up to where the bat lived. The expression on her face became more and more exasperated as she watched powerless as we took one wrong turn after another.

"Take the first turning to the left," a mouse had said from around a corner. But that only led to more halls and more stairs.

"Take the second door to the right," a cockroach had said from behind a thick drape. But that only led to more doors and more rooms.

"Take the third door to the left," a spider had said from the edge of a picture frame. But that only led to more and more frustration.

Finally James said, "I think we've been down this hall before."

"That's not helpful," replied Katherine.

"What? I'm just pointing out the fact that you're lost," said James, "and also that you're stupid," he added.

"Oh, pipe down, James," I interjected, and Katherine used this opportunity to stick her tongue out at him.

"Katherine," I said, "why don't you look outside at Mary. I've been noticing her jumping and twisting out there. Either she has ants in her dress or she's trying to tell us something."

That she was, and through the mysterious wonders of adolescent girl sign language Mary was able to guide Katherine right up to the hall that led to the bat's door.

She tapped politely on it three times. When there was no answer she tapped again three times. When again nothing happened James shoved her aside and pounded loudly on it with his forearm.

"You have been rude, spounding like that," came a tiny voice from high on the door jam. "I shouldn'st swonder if sbat refuses to see yous at all."

"Is that yous, Shcandelaria," asked Katherine in a voice that astonished us.

"You talk to spiders?" oozed James.

"Oh, yes, and are's yous Scasrins?" said the spider sweetly, "sorry, all humans looks alike to me. Anywhats I'll just goes insides and let sbat knows who's you are."

"Sthanks," Katherine called out after her, but she was already long gone through a crack in the door molding.

After a few minutes of waiting and exchanging frustrated looks we three children were admitted to the bat sanctuary and told to sit on the floor. James, however sat in the rocking chair and Katherine had to kick him because he was making the floor squeak.

Finally when it was sufficiently quiet the bat unfurled its wonderful membranous wings and addressed them in a high but dignified voice.

"So you let Mary out, did you?" said the bat looking me dead in the eye.

"Was that wrong?" I asked.

"He's sorry," said James.

"Oh don't be sorry, my friends," said the bat, "this is not the kind of place where humans were meant to live forever."

"Or even for one sday," said Shcandelaria. The bat gave her a beady-eye look and she slunk back into the door molding.

"But most humans, sadly, never leave these kinds of places," he continued, "they remain forever trapped in fantasies of their own making."

"I KNOW," I said, a little too loudly, "can you help me get out?"

"I am just one small bat with a name too hilarious to take seriously."

"What *is* your name, again?" I asked.

"Ivanhoho!"

James stifled a giggle and then laughed out loud. Katherine kicked him.

"Oh, it's quite okay to laugh," said the bat, "I do it myself quite often. None of us should ever take ourselves too seriously. The best way to do that, of course is to have a humorous name or even worse, an obscure family name. I once knew this bat named Mountbatten…"

"Are you ever going to tell us how to get out of here?" James interrupted rudely.

"Unfortunately The Harmony Code tells us that once a person is liberated out of this place through a sacrificial substitution, the liberator becomes himself captured by the very power that trapped the one he liberated."

"We thought we could just smash our way out with Logokrataioo," said James.

"You have Logokrataioo here?" inquired Ivanhoho.

"It's downstairs. Why lug it all the way up here? Do you need to bless it or something?"

"Silly child, a bat's blessing is no better than a boy's. *That* sword is only a symbol of the great El's empowering of His own."

"The rats told me its name means 'WORD POWER' so we thought it was magic. But it didn't work." said James.

"Oh but magic *does work*, yet take heed of its evil source before you become consumed by it."

"So if Logokrataioo doesn't mean 'WORD POWER,'" I said, "what does it mean?"

"It means 'WORD EMPOWERING.' And the term Logo means none other than El Himself. So William, if you are ever to break out from the power of this house, you will have to do it using His strength. But the interesting thing is: He won't simply do all the work for you and you can't make Him do anything against His will."

"So you're saying I'm trapped here forever?" I asked.

"I'm saying nothing of the kind. I'm saying you need to go back downstairs, pick up that sword and talk to El. Work it out with Him. You'll find in life that everything is fully controlled by El and yet you are created with a faculty for independent action. This is a mystery that even bats can't fully fathom."

"So let's get on with it already," said James.

I just sat there, stunned and confused but Katherine rose gracefully to her feet, dusted herself off and curtseyed politely to the bat. "Thank you Mister Ivanhoho. I don't think your name is funny at all. If you should ever get caught in my house I will be sure to show you the easiest way out."

With that the bat furled himself again in his wings and was asleep before the trio had even left the room.

On their way out Shcandelaria intoned in her peculiar, pleading tone, "You're not leaving are you?"

"Most definitely," hissed James, "and the sooner the better."

Going down was easier because Mary was still there at each window to lend guidance by pointing left or right. The miscellaneous animals and insects kept to themselves but followed close by because everyone wanted to see what I would do with that greatsword in the living room.

"Of course, you'll have a spot of tea first," came the familiar voice of Adeylia from the formal dining room. She was putting some scrumptious looking scones on the table, complete with butter curls and several inviting jams and marmalades.

"I'm sorry," began Katherine, but before she could finish James had stuffed six of the biscuits into his pockets and helped himself to three spoonfuls of jelly.

"James you're such a pig," said Katherine and apologized profusely to Adeylia. "So long," she said at last, "I'll certainly miss you."

The mouse tried to frown but couldn't, yet there appeared the unmistakable hint of a tear at her eye.

While all this was going on I had picked up the sword and was quietly saying a prayer to myself... no I didn't exactly do that. I simply spoke to God and said, "Okay Lord, here we go, if you're willing!"

And we did. We didn't even break anything on the way out – except the invisible power keeping me trapped in the mansion. We just walked, blade first, right through the front door. It didn't seem to take any effort at all. But I was careful afterward to give credit where credit was due. "Thank you God," I said out loud.

As soon as I was free I regained my original size and popped up embarrassing close to Mary who was standing at the door waiting for something to happen. In fact I materialized so close to her that we had to cling to each other momentarily to avoid knocking us both over backwards. I guess you could call that sort of a hug, but Mary acted so startled and disgusted that you could hardly call it anything nice at all.

"Excuse me," I said, but she seemed more concerned with the state of her hair and clothes than with me.

Soon, mercifully Katherine appeared with James in tow. He had jelly all over his face.

I did hug Katherine warmly and the four of us beat a hasty retreat out of the room. At the top of the stairs I glanced at Mary, who looked hesitant and fearful. "Well, I guess it's time to introduce you to Aunt Clara." I said, "Won't she be surprised at what we found upstairs!"

~Epilogue~

The rest of the book is history. James never married. I don't suppose any girl in her right mind would have him. He joined the Navy as an ordinary seaman and worked his way all the way up to Lieutenant Commander. He still had a fondness for jelly and had a small collection of swords on his wall.

Katherine did marry and moved away with her husband. They had five children, two girls, a boy who looked just like me, and twin urchins which nobody could tell apart or even be sure they had eyes under all that hair.

Great Aunt Clara lived to be a ripe old age, perhaps even a bit beyond ripe, and died in her sleep one Sunday afternoon. We all gathered at her house for the funeral and were just catching up on all the family news when Katherine's kids came bounding in with exciting news of a dollhouse up on the third floor. One of her urchins had even broken off a weathervane to prove it. James rose to handle the situation, but Katherine sat him back down and motioned us all, including the children to stay put.

Broken weathervane in hand, she went to the roll top desk in the tiny room across from the den, retrieved an old-fashioned key from a drawer, and ascended the stairs with it. She closed and started to lock the door at the top, but thought twice, opened it again and slipped inside. She sat on the bed. Had it all been a dream, she wondered fingering the scar on her arm. She strolled over to Levancrieff Castle but all was quiet inside. Movement in Mousumerset Manor caught her eye, but by the time she got over to peer in, all was still. "Adeylia, Shcandelaria," she called out self-consciously, "Ivanhoho?" but all was still. Then she noticed a toothpick on the floor and instantly knew it was not a toothpick at all, but the magnificent bejeweled greatsword Logokrataioo. Remembering her promise of long ago, she picked it up daintily and laid it gently well inside the castle drawbridge. Strange thing, she reflected, her hand didn't shrink a bit. Perhaps it all had been a fairy tale after all.

She stuck the weathervane back on the mansion and firmly locked the door on the way out. Downstairs she went over to my wife, slipped something into her hand and said, "If you're going to inherit this house, you'd better take better care of this key than Aunt Clara did, especially when my children come to visit."

"Yes Katherine, we will, won't we," I said, glancing into my wife's beautiful green eyes. "We wouldn't want anybody to get trapped."

"No, indeed, we wouldn't," said Mary.

Endnotes:

[1] Rules of Manners adapted from "The Image of Loveliness" by Joanne Wallace, Salem Oregon, c.1978.
[2] Pirate Code adapted from www.nationmaster.com/encyclopedia/Pirate-code-of-the-Brethren.
[3] Ten Commandments of Chivalry adapted from www.astro.umd.edu/~marshall/chivalry.html.
[4] Ten Principles of Charm adapted from "The Image of Loveliness" by Joanne Wallace, Salem Oregon, c.1978.

Ecclesiastes 9:12

No one knows what will happen next.
Like a fish caught in a net,
or a bird caught in a trap,
people are **trapped** by evil
when it suddenly falls on them.

The Holy Bible
New Century Version

www.ingramcontent.com/pod-product-compliance
Lightning Source LLC
Chambersburg PA
CBHW030522260626
47157CB00005B/1841